Skye just wasn't prepared for her cousin's request

Jodi declared excitedly. "Skye, I want you to paint a portrait of Thane for me—as our wedding present."

Skye's face paled as she stared at her cousin in consternation. "Oh, but I couldn't. It's impossible. A portrait takes a long time." She was terrified at the thought of spending so many hours alone with the man she yearned for. She protested, "And maybe Thane doesn't want to waste hours sitting for his portrait."

Then Thane spoke, in a tone that brought Skye's eyes to his face. "Of course I'll sit for it. But perhaps Skye doesn't want to paint my picture."

Unsteadily, she answered, "Of course I—I want to paint you."

Thane's eyes held hers as he said, "Good, that's settled, then...."

SALLY WENTWORTH began her publishing career at a Fleet Street newspaper in London, where she thrived in the hectic atmosphere. After her marriage, she and her husband moved to rural Hertfordshire, where Sally had been raised. Although she worked for the publisher of a group of magazines, the day soon came when her own writing claimed her energy and time.

Books by Sally Wentworth

Don't miss any of our special offers. Write to us at the following address for information on our newest releases.

Harlequin Reader Service
901 Fuhrmann Blvd., P.O. Box 1397, Buffalo, NY 14240
Canadian address: P.O. Box 603,
Fort Erie, Ont. L2A 5X3

SALLY WENTWORTH

wish on the moon

Harlequin Books

TORONTO • NEW YORK • LONDON
AMSTERDAM • PARIS • SYDNEY • HAMBURG
STOCKHOLM • ATHENS • TOKYO • MILAN

Harlequin Presents first edition June 1990
ISBN 0-373-11278-5

Original hardcover edition published in 1989
by Mills & Boon Limited

CHAPTER ONE

SKYE HOLMAN looked up from the letter she was reading and exclaimed, 'Good heavens! Jodi wants me to be a bridesmaid at her wedding.'

'Who's Jodi?' her mother murmured absently as she read the morning paper. 'One of your art college friends?'

Skye smiled. 'No, she's your niece, Jodi Benton.'

Mrs Holman looked up with a frown. 'Her name isn't Jodi, it's Judy. You must have read it wrongly.'

'No, don't you remember?' Skye explained patiently. 'She decided Judy was too dull and old-fashioned, so she changed it to Jodi when she was still at school. She thought it sounded more with it.'

'Judith is a perfectly good name,' her mother remarked. 'I seem to remember she was named after her grandmother.'

'Well, whatever her name, she wants me to be a bridesmaid. But the wedding is to be in the West Indies and in only two months' time, so it's quite out of the question, of course. Trust Jodi to just expect you to drop everything and go running when she calls.'

Her mother took off her glasses and gave Skye her full attention. 'What exactly does she say?'

Picking up the letter, Skye gave a verbal précis. 'She says she's going to marry this absolutely fabulous New York lawyer. The wedding will take place

5

in Nassau, on New Providence Island, and we're all invited. And, as I said, she wants me to go out there as soon as I possibly can so that I can have a dress made and be a bridesmaid.'

'Well, I don't think for a minute that we'll be able to get your father to go,' Mrs Holman said resignedly. 'You know what he's like about flying. But James might like to attend. He was quite fond of Judy, I seem to remember.'

'Jodi,' Skye corrected. 'Yes, they used to get on well, but then James got that roving-reporter job, and Jodi and her parents went to live in the West Indies, so they haven't seen a great deal of each other since then.'

'Well, I'll pass the invitation on to James next time I write,' Mrs Holman said, then she looked at her daughter keenly. 'Why don't you go? It will do you good to get some sun and rest after your operation.'

'Oh, Mum, having your appendix out is nothing nowadays. I'll soon be fine.'

'But they only just caught it in time, and you're still very weak. A convalescent holiday in the sun will do wonders for you. I think you ought to go,' she was told firmly.

Skye looked at her mother in foreboding; when she spoke in that particular tone it was a sure sign that she'd made up her mind, and once it was made up, very little would shake it. 'But I have my work to do,' she protested. 'You know I have that greetings card contract to complete. And I'm waiting to hear if I've got those book illustrations to do. I can't possibly go away. I've lost enough time by being in hospital.'

'Nonsense,' she was told roundly. 'You're just making excuses. If the work is so urgent, you can take your equipment with you to the West Indies and do it there. John and Helen won't mind,' she added, naming Jodi's parents.

'But you know what Jodi's like,' Skye protested. 'She never stands still for a minute and she'll expect me to go everywhere with her. I won't have any time to rest, let alone work.'

'You will when they know you've been ill. I shall phone them up today and tell them.'

'Mother!' Skye wailed. 'I haven't said I want to go. I won't know anyone.'

'Then it will give you a good opportunity to meet people, won't it?' her mother said heartlessly. 'And of course you want to go—what girl wouldn't?'

Skye tried to make her mother listen to her, but knew when she was beaten. For ninety-nine per cent of the time Anne Holman was easy-going to the point of indifference, allowing her family to lead their own lives and completely engrossed in her own, but that other one per cent of the time, when she made up her mind about something, she became totally implacable and trying to argue or persuade her otherwise was just a waste of time and energy. And besides, although Skye was concerned about her work, the idea of being a bridesmaid, and in such an exotic place, appealed to her imagination. Also, the operation *had* left her feeling as weak as a kitten, and it would be marvellous to get away from the current spell of wet weather in England and go to the sun. So in no time at all it was arranged that she would fly to Nassau as soon as she was strong enough. 'And I'll try and come out there with James for the wedding,' Anne Holman promised. 'Although if that concert at the Barbican clashes with the date, I shall go to that instead.'

They were a creative family, the Holmans; her parents had met because both their careers were in music, her father a composer and arranger and her mother a cellist. But with Skye the creative streak had been for painting, and she had become an artist. In her brother James it had been writing, and he was rapidly making a name for himself as a journalist. Their respective careers meant that they were often apart, and Skye and James had been looked after in their childhood by a succession of nannies and mother's helps, but they were a close family for all that, and thoroughly enjoyed the brief periods when they were all together in their rambling old house in the English countryside.

Skye had a large room over the garage converted into a studio and spent most of her time there, but over the next two weeks, as her strength gradually returned, her mother became uncharacteristically strict and would only allow her to work there for an hour or so at a time before she rested again. Even so, Skye managed to get quite a lot of the background research work done for the greetings cards she had been commissioned to do, and she didn't have to pack too much equipment when she finally got ready to leave for Nassau.

Her father drove her to the airport and gave her firm instructions about not attempting to carry her cases herself. 'Get a porter,' he urged her.

'Yes, all right, Dad. Don't worry, I'll be fine.'

But, despite her protestations, Skye was more than glad to finally land at Nassau Airport. She had had to change planes in Miami, and although she hadn't had to handle her luggage, she and the other transferring passengers had had to stand in line for a long time to get seats on the next flight, and then there had been the Customs, too. She found a smiling porter for her two suitcases and followed him out into the main concourse, then paused for a moment, slightly confused by the throngs of people.

'There she is! Skye! Over here.' And hurrying towards her came both Jodi and her aunt Helen.

They greeted her effusively, even though they hadn't seen each other for about four years. Both of the women looked slim and chic, her aunt in a summer dress and Jodi in more casual but equally expensive clothes.

'You've grown!' Jodi exclaimed. 'I always thought you were shorter than me. But never mind, you'll be some way behind me at the wedding.'

'You can tell Skye all about the wedding later,' Aunt Helen interrupted, seeing the tiredness in Skye's face. 'I'm sure she'd like to go home now and have a rest. Don't forget she's been ill.'

'I'm fine. Just a little tired from the journey.'

But her aunt put a hand under Skye's elbow and led her out of the shady airport building into the brilliant light of a West Indian afternoon. Skye blinked, dazzled by the sun, but lifted her face to its enveloping warmth.

'The car's over here.'

Skye blinked again when she saw the car. It was a long American convertible in apple-green, with leather seats in a paler shade. It was so wide that they could all three have sat in the front, but her aunt came in the back with her while Jodi drove.

'You drive on the left-hand side of the road,' Skye remarked in surprise. 'I thought you'd drive on the right.'

'No. Don't forget that the Bahamas were British for over three hundred years. The only trouble is that most of the cars are imported from the United States, so the steering wheels are on the wrong side.'

As they drove along Aunt Helen pointed out all the places of interest, which mostly seemed to consist of country clubs, golf clubs and, as they drew nearer the sea, marinas and beaches. But Skye was fascinated by the light and the colours, her fingers itching to get hold of a brush and some paint. There were such vivid contrasts in the sky and the trees, some of them full of rich red flowers. And the people too wore such bright, happy colours. Skye could have set up her easel at almost every point they passed. The road went through the outskirts of Nassau town, down to the sea, and then followed the coast for a while until Jodi turned up a road that rose along the side of a hill, a place where trees partly hid luxurious houses on either side. After a few minutes Jodi swung into the driveway of one of these and pulled up in front of a beautiful colonnaded house, a southern plantation house in miniature, with a balcony running all round the upper floor.

'What do you think of it?' her aunt asked.

Skye realised she was being asked to praise, and could answer sincerely, 'It's a lovely house. Exactly right for its setting.'

Her aunt seemed pleased and ushered her inside, into a sitting-room with windows looking out over the hillside to the sea. Immediately outside was a terrace set with loungers and garden chairs, and with steps leading down to lawns and a swimming pool, the whole surrounded by similar richly flowering trees and shrubs as those Skye had noticed during the drive from the airport. Tomorrow, she thought, I'll find out the names of all the trees. But right now she was glad to sit down in a chair and accept the long, cool drink that her aunt offered her.

'Thank you. How is Uncle John? Is he working?'

'Yes, he's in New York at the moment, but he'll be flying down at the weekend with Thane and Scott. And Thane's sister is coming down in a few weeks. She's another of the bridesmaids.'

'I take it Thane is Jodi's fiancé? You didn't tell us his name in your letter, only that he was fabulous,' she told her cousin with a smile.

'Didn't I?' Jodi came to sit beside her and said animatedly, 'His name is Thane Tyson, and he's a lawyer with a well-known firm in New York. He's thirty years old and he's tall and fair and gorgeous.'

Skye laughed. 'You're right, he does sound fabulous, but maybe you're biased. And who is Scott?'

'Oh, that's Scott McGee, Thane's closest friend. They were at law school together and now they work for the same firm. And Scott is going to be best man at the wedding.'

'That's enough for now,' Aunt Helen warned as Jodi was about to continue. 'Why don't you take

Skye up to her room so that she can rest before dinner?'

There were wide stairs leading up to a landing that went all round the house, and Skye's room was at the side, looking out over the gardens, with only a glimpse of the sea unless you went out on to the balcony. But it was a very pretty room with the curtains, carpet and bed-hangings all toning with the basic pale lemon colour, as were the towels and suite in the adjoining bathroom. Skye was sure it was tastefully done, and it was certainly very luxurious, but she felt rather as if she'd stepped into an illustration in a 'Perfect Homes for Plutocrats' magazine. Everything was so matching, so contrived. Not like her room back home, where the furniture was mainly antique items from a variety of periods which had been bought at auction sales, the curtains batik-dyed and made herself when she'd been at art college, and the bedspread a patchwork quilt made from old dresses by her mother when she'd had to rest after slipping on the ice and breaking her leg one winter. Rather a hotch-potch when you compared it to this decorator-designed room, but Skye was quite sure which she preferred.

'Why, the maid hasn't unpacked for you!' Jodi exclaimed when she saw Skye's suitcase on the floor.

'Oh, no, please—those are my painting things.'

'That's right, I remember you take them with you everywhere, don't you?' Jodi looked at her curiously. 'You're making a career out of painting, aren't you? Are you successful?'

Skye gave her slow smile and, kicking off her shoes, lay down on the bed. 'Shall we say, I'm making slow but steady progress? I have a lot of competition.'

'What do you do exactly?'

'I'm a freelance. I do anything I'm asked. Illustrations for children's books, advertisements, book covers, greetings cards, anything like that.'

'Don't you do proper paintings—portraits and things?'

'In my spare time, or when I run out of work. Although then I'm usually touting round to try to get more commissions. The bread and butter work has to come first, you see.'

Jodi frowned and said with the tactless freedom of a relation, 'But your parents aren't hard up, are they? Won't they support you so that you can paint what you like?'

'Possibly. But I prefer to be independent.'

Her cousin's finely arched brows rose in surprise and incomprehension. She was the only child of very rich parents and had been indulged all her life. Added to which, both her parents were ambitious and trendy, seeking out the best of material things in life and teaching their daughter to do the same. Jodi knew everything there was to know about fashion, décor and the latest trends, but would have been aghast at the idea of earning her own living. She was like a pretty doll, Skye thought, brought up to do nothing but enjoy herself and be a loved adornment, first for her parents, and then for the man she was going to marry, the lawyer from New York, Thane Tyson. Skye wondered what he was like, whether he was materialistic too. From what she had read about American lawyers, they were mostly rich, or on the way to being rich, anyway.

'Do you think James will be able to come to the wedding?' Jodi asked. 'I haven't seen him in ages.'

'Mother has written to tell him he's invited, but he's in West Africa at the moment, reporting on the drought there. We don't see very much of him ourselves; he's usually only home a few days before he gets sent on another assignment.'

'Is he OK? And your parents, of course?'

Skye gave Jodi a quick glance, remembering the crush she'd had on James when they were children. 'He's fine. Last time he came home he was terrifically tanned. Almost as brown as you,' she remarked, looking at Jodi's deep tan.

'You'll soon get brown yourself once you get into the sun. At the moment you look as if you've been shut inside for months,' the other girl observed, looking at Skye's pale skin.

'I feel that way. The weather in England has been terrible this year, but of course there was a mini heatwave while I was shut up in hospital.'

Jodi laughed and stood up. 'I'd better let you rest now or Mother will tell me off. Dinner is at eight, so I'll come and wake you around seven, shall I?'

Skye thanked her, and when Jodi had gone, stood up to take off her skirt and blouse. She caught sight of herself in the full-length mirror and thought how different she and Jodi looked, even though they were cousins. Jodi was so fair and quite petite really, although she liked to think she was tall and always wore very high heels. She was quite curvy too, whereas Skye was tall and very slender, and had an unruly mane of dark hair that framed a sensitive, fine-boned face and large, dark eyes, smoky eyes that often had a dreamy quality about them, as if her inner thoughts were far more engrossing than the world outside.

But it was in their personalities that the biggest differences lay. Jodi was, like her mother, a hive of nervous energy, always looking for some new entertainment, and wanting to be among people, the more the better, and if it was a party that was better still. Skye too, enjoyed the occasional party, but much preferred them when they grew out of an impromptu gathering of friends rather than a set date with everyone dressed up and feeling that they must eat and drink a lot to have a good time. And Skye derived immense pleasure and contentment from her painting, and could happily spend an hour just looking at a view or a flower before she even started to paint it, but Jodi would have been bored within minutes if she was made to sit still for long.

After her nap, Skye had dinner with Jodi and her aunt, and then went with them to visit friends nearby. The next day they took her on a tour of the island and were surprised when she was more interested in the names of flowers and trees than those of the owners of rich houses and estates. They went to a fashionable golf club for lunch, to a pseudo-native bar for cocktails and to a seafood restaurant for dinner. The following day they went out on the Bentons' luxury motor-yacht with some friends of Jodi's for a sail round the island, and in the evening they went to a nightclub.

It was all so different, and Skye found it enjoyable. Jodi's friends were around their own age and they made her welcome, but there was something almost frenetic about the way they went all

out to enjoy themselves that she found completely
alien to her nature, so she pleaded tiredness and
went home ahead of the others.

Friday was the day that Uncle John and Jodi's
fiancé and his friend were due to arrive. They were
flying down and were due to reach Nassau in the
early evening. Skye expected Jodi to go and meet
them, but it was Aunt Helen who drove out to the
airport because Jodi was late getting back from
having her hair done. She ran upstairs to change
and Skye followed her, putting on a soft full skirt
and matching long-sleeved top in a pale lilac colour.
All her life she had been taught that looks were far
less important than talent; she knew she looked OK
and the colour suited her, but she had no idea of
the ephemeral quality she possessed and which was
enhanced by the softness of the dress. She added
a little make-up and, because shades of colour came
naturally to her, knew just what to choose and how
much to use to enhance her high cheekbones and
dark, pensive eyes.

She was ready ahead of Jodi and went to sit out
on the balcony for a while, but soon heard a car
draw up at the front of the house and curiously
walked to the angle of the balcony to have a look.
It was the big green convertible with three men
inside and Aunt Helen at the wheel. As Skye
watched, standing in the shadow of the wall, the
men got out and waited for the boy to take their
bags from the boot. Uncle John she recognised at
once, although his hair had a feather of grey now.
The other two men were superficially very similar.
Both around thirty, both tall and with fairish hair,
and both dressed, like Uncle John, in dark business

suits, evidently having travelled straight from their offices.

Skye looked at the two men, trying to pick out which one was Jodi's fiancé. Presumably the one who was standing talking to her aunt and uncle while the other helped the houseboy to unload the bags. The former was the slightly taller of the two and had the keen features and thrusting jaw of a man who was determined on going places, the clean-cut good looks and short blond hair that was so typical of young American men. He was lean, too, and used his hands to gesticulate in a superfluity of energy as he talked. He would be exactly right for Jodi, Sky judged, both of them being energetic and ambitious. They would make a good team. She could imagine them in the future: Thane a really successful lawyer, perhaps even going into politics, with Jodi not only behind him but probably pushing him every step of the way. And so long as he kept going up the ladder they would both be very happy.

Having satisfied herself on the suitability of her cousin's choice, Skye turned her attention to the best man, Scott McGee. Although the two men were superficially so similar, Skye found that this man interested her much more. He wasn't as wiry as Thane, his shoulders were wider and his chest deeper, but there was an air of contained strength about him. He didn't waste his energy on unnecessary gestures, but seemed very relaxed, standing waiting for the others to finish their conversation in a quiet, almost detached manner. To Skye's artistic eye he had a far more interesting face, too. Perhaps not so conventionally handsome as Thane's, because it was slightly fuller, not so clean-cut, but he had a cleft in his chin that spoke of a sense of humour, and long-lashed dark eyes that hid his thoughts. It was a face she would like to paint. As she looked at him, Skye felt a stirring of something more than artistic interest. She felt that there could be depths to this man's character, that he might be something more than merely ambitious, and that it might be worthwhile getting to know him better.

As if he felt her eyes on him, Scott glanced up and saw her on the balcony. His eyebrows rose in surprise and she felt suddenly shy. She would have stepped back, but Uncle John happened to turn and saw her too. He immediately waved and called out to her, 'Hello, Skye. Glad you could make it. See you shortly.'

Skye waved back and watched as they all went inside, then turned and walked back to her own room. But once there she felt strangely restless. She checked her appearance again, perhaps with a little more thoroughness this time, because it would be nice if she made as favourable an impression on Scott as he had on her. Then she went down the wide staircase, into the sitting-room, and through the french windows on to the terrace. The sun was just beginning to set. Skye walked to the edge of the terrace and leaned against the rail as she looked out across the beach to the sea. The air was full of the most exotic scents. A thousand fragrances, far more beautiful than any manufactured perfume she had ever smelt, drifted on the slight breeze from the gardens all around. So this is the real Caribbean, she thought, not the hundreds of hotels and shops, not the golf clubs or luxury marinas, but this beautiful, exotic scent that steals into your senses, and the gold of the sky reflected on the rippling waves of the sea. A rich blaze of colour that was indescribably lovely and ate into her heart, making her feel that she could never pick up a brush and try to paint again, for no artist in the world, however gifted, could even attempt to paint the beauty and magnificence of that sky.

She stood on the terrace for a long time, completely lost in the sunset, and didn't hear someone else coming out until a man's voice behind her said, 'It's really something, isn't it?'

As Scott came up beside her, Skye half turned her head and nodded. 'I think it's one of the most magnificent sights I've ever seen,' she answered simply. 'It tears at my heart and makes me feel unbelievably sad and at the same time immensely grateful.'

Scott turned to look at her with open interest in his eyes. 'Why does it make you feel that way?'

'Sad because it reminds me of my own mortality, but grateful that I'm alive at all and have been privileged to see it, I suppose. Doesn't it make you feel that way, too?'

'Every time,' he agreed. 'A Caribbean sunset isn't something you take for granted, no matter how many times you see it. And it doesn't matter how often you try to photograph it, you can never really capture the essence of a sunset. You can show the beauty of it, perhaps, but never the way it makes you feel when you actually see it.'

'It's the same with paint,' Skye said warmly. 'I don't think anyone has come near really setting that feeling down on canvas. But then, feelings are difficult.'

Scott moved round a little to lean back against the terrace railing. The sunset profiled his features and Skye saw that she had been right about his face; there was definite strength there, hidden under the outward good humour of lazy eyes and an easy smile. This man, too, she thought, could go a long way if he chose. Perhaps even further than Thane, for everyone could see at a glance that Thane intended to get where he wanted to go, but Scott had a natural charm which would win him more friends—and perhaps lull his enemies or rivals into thinking him a lesser man than he was.

She realised that he was studying her too, but he smiled and said, 'I remember now—Jodi said you were artistic.'

Skye laughed, imagining how Jodi would say it, half disparaging, half boasting. 'So I'm condemned unseen.'

He gave her a quick, shrewd glance, then shook his head. 'Not so. Do you know Jodi very well?'

'I used to when they lived in England. We're the same age and our families were together quite a lot because we lived near each other. But our parents had completely different interests so they made other friends and drifted apart, and then Aunt Helen and Uncle John moved out here because Uncle John found that he was doing more business in America than Europe.'

'Who is your actual relation, John or Helen?'

'Uncle John. He's my mother's brother.'

'You and Jodi aren't very much alike,' Scott commented.

'No, we're entirely different, but we get along OK.'

Scott gave a slightly crooked smile. 'I meant in looks.'

'Oh.' Skye felt herself flushing a little and was glad of the shadows. 'No, we're not alike in that, either.' To change the subject she said quickly, 'It must be very different for you here after New York. Like another world.'

He nodded. 'It's starting to heat up there now. A lot of people have left for the coast already. Yes, it's good to get away, even for a couple of days. And there's so much to do here: lots of water-sports, that kind of thing.'

Yes, he would be good at sport, Skye realised as she saw the outline of firm muscles beneath the white dinner-jacket he was wearing. Under it he wore a white shirt but no tie; instead it was un-buttoned at the neck for this most casual of holiday islands.

During the time they had been talking, the sun had sunk much lower in the sky and they both tacitly turned to watch as it clung to the horizon as if afraid to let it go, the sky aflame as the battle was fought. And then the sun was suddenly gone, carrying on its eternal benefaction to another land.

Skye gave a long sigh of mingled loss and en-richment. 'How lucky the people are who live here.'

Scott grinned. 'They probably don't even notice it. If you're brought up with beauty, you don't re-alise you have it until it's taken away from you or you have something else to compare it to. Then you hunger for it.'

As he spoke, Skye looked at him with renewed curiosity. She wondered how he could bear to work and live in New York when he was so appreciative of natural beauty. Surely there were other, more congenial places he could have chosen? She found that she was intrigued by him. She wanted to know more. These few minutes alone had made that first stirring of interest grow. And she was aware of him physically, too. Of his broad shoulders and the strong column of his neck. Of his hands, and the cleft in his chin that hid the determination in his jawline. She felt the beginning of an excitement that she had felt with few other men, an inner knowledge that this just might lead to something. That it was even possible he could turn out to be a man she could fall in love and want to spend the rest of her life with.

Behind them there was the sound of voices in the sitting-room and the terrace lights were turned on. Scott straightened up and turned to smile at Skye. 'Shall we . . .' he began, but the words died in his throat.

Skye was smiling back at him, her face alight with the inner joy of her discovery, her eyes warm and happy. 'I'm so glad that we've met, Scott,' she said simply.

His eyes widened, an arrested expression in their dark depths as he grew suddenly still. Then he gave a short sigh, but before he could speak, Jodi came hurrying out on to the terrace. 'So you two have met!' she exclaimed. 'That's wonderful.' Slipping her arm through Scott's she reached up to kiss him. 'Hello, darling. Sorry I wasn't down earlier. Daddy wants you to give him your opinion of a bottle of wine he's waiting to uncork.'

Scott nodded and gave Skye a swift glance before going into the sitting-room. As soon as he'd gone inside, Jodi ran over to Skye and said excitedly, 'Well, what do you think? Isn't he gorgeous?'

Skye laughed. 'Let me have a real look at Thane first. I only saw him for a few minutes from the balcony.'

They had moved towards the open french windows where she could see into the sitting-room, but now Jodi stood still and looked at her in puzzlement. 'But you've been talking to him.'

'Oh, no, that was Scott. I . . .' Skye stopped as the truth hit her, and with it an appalling rush of deep disappointment.

Jodi realised what had happened at the same moment and gave a peal of laughter. 'You've mixed them up! That was Thane. How crazy. Wait till I tell him.' She paused, and then said, 'Well? What do you think of him?'

Skye looked through the open doorway and into Thane's eyes as he turned towards them. 'You're right,' she said slowly. 'He is gorgeous.' And then steeled herself to go inside.

CHAPTER TWO

UNCLE JOHN immediately came forward to greet Skye and ask after his sister and the rest of the family. He seemed happy enough, although he looked older than Skye remembered: his hair was much thinner and there were frown lines between his brows. They talked for a few minutes before Aunt Helen came over and said, 'You mustn't monopolise her, John. Skye hasn't been introduced to Scott yet.'

Putting a hand on her arm, her aunt led Skye across the room to where the two younger men were talking to Jodi. They broke off their conversation as the two women approached, and turned towards them. Skye looked at Jodi's animated face and then at Scott as Aunt Helen introduced him.

Scott said, 'Hi, Skye.' And then grinned because it sounded so silly. 'Glad to meet you.' He held out his hand and shook hers warmly.

'And of course you've met Thane,' Jodi broke in, and, turning to her fiancé added, 'Why didn't you tell Skye who you were? She had the idea you were Scott.'

'You must have told her you were engaged to the good-looking one,' Scott cut in before Thane could speak. 'And, not being besotted like you, Skye saw clearly that *I'm* the best-looking.'

'For a lawyer, you leave yourself wide open to argument,' Thane remarked. 'No girl in her right mind would think you good-looking.'

Scott began to argue back, and under cover of their banter Skye was able to laugh and gloss over her mistake. She felt an idiot, and wondered now why she'd been so sure that Thane was Scott. Wishful thinking, perhaps? Or was it because she had believed it impossible for her to have felt such an instant liking for someone who was already engaged? But, whichever it was, she had been stupid to have made the liking known, let alone before she was even sure who she was talking to. Scott asked her some questions about England and her trip, but then she turned to speak to her uncle as he came up to join them.

'Do you think your parents and James will be able to get here for the wedding?' he asked her.

'I don't know about Dad, but Mum says she will if she can. There's a concert coming up in London, you see, and she might be asked to take part.'

For a moment, Uncle John looked annoyed. 'Anne always did put her music first. Even before her husband and children. Every time we came to see you there was a different person looking after you and James.' Skye merely looked at him serenely and he gave a rueful grin. 'I must admit, though, that it doesn't seem to have done you any harm. And you always seemed happy enough.'

Relenting at that, Skye said, 'I'm afraid creative people do tend to be selfish. Mum has a great talent and she didn't see why she should give it up to bring up her children when she could employ people who would do it as well, if not better.'

He laughed and said, 'Now, I wonder where you heard that?' But then he looked at his daughter with loving pride. 'Each to his own, I suppose, but I could never have let Jodi be brought up like that.'

Overhearing his remark, Scott turned and clapped him on the shoulder. 'You and Mrs Benton did a great job, sir.'

Uncle John looked pleased, but Skye was rather surprised; she felt that if anyone should have made that remark it should have been Thane, who must also have heard it. Personally she thought it rather a fulsome and unnecessary compliment, but maybe Thane did too and that was why he hadn't made it. He was standing with Jodi now, telling her about some relations of his who couldn't make it to the wedding. Jodi had her arm linked through his and was listening to what he said, but she had heard Scott's compliment and turned to flash him a smile, and her eyes kept drifting away from Thane to see what everyone else was doing.

Skye watched them under her lashes, wondering how long they'd been together and how well they knew each other.

A clock in the room struck eight, and exactly on the last chime Uncle John said, 'Ah, dinner!' and opened the door to lead them into the dining-room. Skye was placed between her uncle and Scott with Jodi immediately opposite and Thane next to her cousin, with Aunt Helen presiding at the other end of the table.

Scott evidently felt that it was his job to entertain her, because he turned to Skye immediately they sat down and asked her if she'd ever been to America before.

'Only to California and Florida for holidays.'

'How about New York?'

She shook her head. 'No, I've never been there.'

'Hey, do you hear that?' Scott addressed the whole table. 'Skye has never visited the Big Apple. You'll have to do something about that, Jodi. We can't let her go home without seeing New York.'

'She'll have to go there anyway,' Jodi replied casually, 'to have her bridesmaid's dress fitted. They're all being made by a store in Fifth Avenue,' she explained.

This was news to Skye, who hadn't begun to think about her dress. 'When do you intend to go?' she asked.

'Don't worry,' Aunt Helen broke in. 'We'll give you time to recover from your operation a little more before we all fly to New York.'

Thane turned to look at Skye. 'Have you been ill?'

It was the first time he'd addressed her directly since they'd come in from the terrace, since she'd known who he really was, and she answered a little more sharply than she'd intended. 'Not really. It was only an appendix operation.'

'But you're looking very pale. Don't you think so, Scott? We must all take care of her and make sure that Skye rests as much as she can,' Aunt Helen said.

'Sure thing,' Scott agreed with his usual enthusiasm. 'Don't worry, Mrs Benton, I'll make it my personal responsibility to make sure Skye doesn't overdo it.'

'Thank you, Scott. You hear, Skye? Scott has promised to take care of you,' she said with a laugh.

Skye smiled rather hollowly and wished they would change the subject. She didn't feel like an invalid and didn't want to be treated as one. And she wasn't sure that she particularly liked the thought of Scott appointing himself as her keeper; she had an idea that his guardianship might be a whole lot more exhausting than resting at home.

Perhaps something of what she was thinking showed in her face, because she glanced up and caught a quirk of amusement at the corner of Thane's mouth. Her own lips twitched in response but then were quickly still as she looked away, remembering that she had no right to feel such empathy with Thane. Her heart beating a little unevenly, Skye turned to her uncle and concentrated on talking to him for the next few minutes. When she eventually looked back at the others she saw that they were all talking together, so it was safe to relax. She mentally chided herself on being so sensitive; it had been simply a case of mistaken identity, that was all. Thane had probably forgotten the whole thing by now. Or he would have if she hadn't blurted out that impulsive remark about being glad they'd met. But it had been so long since she'd met a man with whom she'd felt such an immediate rapport that she had let it show. And Thane had noticed all right; he was far too acute not to have done. And maybe he had felt the rapport too.

They were discussing their plans for the weekend. Windsurfing, sailing, a cruise in the motor-yacht to another island, a round of golf, dinner at the casino and taking in the floorshow. All these things were suggested, until Skye wondered how they were going to cram everything in. Life here seemed to be lived at an entirely different pace than she was used to. She thought they had done quite a lot in the days since she had been here, but evidently that had been only idling the time away; with the coming of the men and the weekend, the pace of the 'restful life' was really getting under way.

Listening to them, Skye realised that Scott tended to monopolise the conversation, looking round at them all to hold their eyes and make sure they were listening to him, raising his voice slightly if he thought they were drifting away. But he was up against another assertive man in Uncle John, who could snatch the conversational ball from him whenever he wanted to—or did Scott tactfully let him? However, Thane could do it too, both subtly with some oblique remark or just by saying, 'Hey, don't you ever stop acting as if you're in a courtroom?'

As Skye watched them, she wondered about the two men, about their friendship when their personalities seemed so different, but most of all she wondered about Thane and Jodi and whether they were in love. And, if they were, why was there no current of excitement between them? None of that magnetism that was so strong between lovers that it could be felt by other people in the room? Jodi touched Thane a lot, putting her hand on his arm and leaning against his shoulder, but to Skye it seemed to be more possessiveness than love, a way of saying, Look, he's mine. And they didn't look into each other's eyes, the rest of the world forgotten, as she had seen other lovers do. Did that mean that they knew each other very well, that they

were old lovers in every sense of the word? Had
the magic faded so much? Perhaps it had, perhaps
that was what they had waited for before they decided to marry: sureness of love that had outlasted
sexual excitement.

After dinner, Jodi suggested they all go to a
nightclub, so they all six piled into the green convertible to drive over to Paradise Island and the
Ocean Club. Uncle John drove this time, with Skye
next to him and Scott on her other side, with the
others in the rear seat. The sunset had given way
to a beautiful night with the warmth of velvet. As
they neared the town the streets became full of
traffic, and pedestrians thronged the pavements.
Everyone seemed to be on the move and there was
a hubbub of noise all around. Skye looked about
her in fascination, enjoying the noise and the bustle,
the music that sounded from the open doorways of
bars and the people who jigged along the street in
time to the music, smiling and colourful. They had
to queue to pay the toll to go across the bridge, and
then followed a line of taxis until they turned right
off the main road and left the cabs behind.

'Where are they all going?' Skye asked.

'To the casino, I guess. There must be a couple
of cruise ships in the harbour,' Scott answered, then
looked to Uncle John for confirmation. 'Is that
right, sir?'

'I expect so.'

They turned up a narrow, tree-lined driveway and
soon drew up in the covered entrance-way of a pale
pink Georgian-style mansion. A doorman in old-
fashioned livery opened the door for them, while
a boy waited to drive the car away and park it. The

beguiling notes of a jazz band met them as they crossed the polished floor of the entrance hall and went up the gently curved staircase. It was New Orleans jazz. They sat down to listen, sipping rum-based drinks in long glasses with tiny paper parasols and parrots and stirring-sticks added to the fruit in them until you could hardly see the liquid.

Scott sat next to Skye and began to talk to her, but she merely nodded because she wanted to listen to the music, so he turned to talk to Jodi instead. All too soon the jazz band stopped playing and made way for a modern group, all electric instruments, freaky hairstyles and tight trousers.

'Great!' Jodi exclaimed. 'Now we'll be able to dance.' And she jumped on to the floor and pulled Thane after her.

'Let's go, Skye.' Scott too got to his feet and held out his hand to her.

'Sorry, I'm afraid it's too fast for me at the moment. But, please, go ahead and dance with someone else.'

'Say, that's right, I forgot.' He sat down again beside her, but moved his body in time to the music, and when her aunt and uncle got up to dance he looked restlessly round. 'You sure you don't mind?' And before Skye could answer he had gone to ask a girl sitting across the room to dance.

Skye watched the gyrating couples for a while, smiling as she saw the older generation letting their hair down. They danced well, too. But her eyes were drawn to where Jodi and Thane danced together. Jodi was really gone, her body moving with a jerky gracefulness, her eyes half closed as she let the music take hold. Thane moved easily enough, enjoying himself, but not as gone as Jodi. His eyes moved round the room, over the other dancers who swayed beneath the swiftly changing lights, past the people sitting at the tables—and came to Skye. His gaze settled on her and he smiled. Skye smiled back, but the smile didn't come naturally this time, she had to force herself to make it a social smile without any trace of the liking she felt. And then they both looked away, Thane to let his glance travel on, and Skye down to her drink. Scott seemed to be getting on well with the girl he was dancing with, a thin blonde with long hair fastened with a huge red plastic clip.

Skye put down her drink, slipped out of the darkened, pulsating room and made her way out into the open and the garden that surrounded the club. The moonlit gardens were beautiful: stretching out before her were grassed terraces bounded by stone walls, and with bronze statues standing in shaded niches. You could almost believe that you were in the garden of some nineteenth-century mansion or French château, Skye thought as she strolled slowly along. Or at least you could if it wasn't for the echoing beat of that very twentieth-century music.

She found a stone bench and sat down, thinking that she must come and see this place in the daylight; it must look very beautiful when the masses of flowers and shrubs that she could see now as only paler shades of grey showed their true, magnificent colours.

It must have been only ten minutes or so since she'd left the club when Skye heard footsteps coming along the stone path and a masculine voice calling her name.

'Over here,' she answered, and felt a little frisson of pleasure when she saw that it was Thane who'd come in search of her.

'Hi. You OK? Helen sent me to find you.'

'That was nice of her. But I'm fine really, I just needed to get some fresh air.'

'Was it too hot for you in there?'

Skye laughed. 'No, actually it was chilly; I haven't got used to the sudden change in temperature that you get with air-conditioning yet.'

Thane's eyebrows rose. 'I hadn't thought of that one. I guess we're all immune to extreme changes. In winter we go from freezing cold to high central-heating, and in summer from unbearable heat to the cool of air-conditioning.'

'I wonder you survive,' she said lightly, but then stood up, belatedly—after that first moment of pleasure—remembering she had no right to monopolise his company.

'Why don't you take a little longer to warm up?' Apparently in no hurry to go in, Thane raised his head to look around him. 'They call these the Versailles Gardens; they're said to be a copy of the gardens round the château in France. Say, have you ever been there?'

Skye nodded. 'Yes, several times. Have you?'

'No, but it's one of the places Jodi and I intend to take in on our honeymoon trip. Are these gardens the same?'

Again a feeling of desolation filled her as Skye thought of him on honeymoon with Jodi, but she managed to nod and say, 'Via Hollywood, perhaps. Where else are you going?'

Thane laughed and shrugged. 'Where *aren't* we going? The list seems to get longer every day; there are so many places that Jodi wants to show me.'

'Yes, I can imagine she might,' Skye agreed, thinking how wonderful it must be to show the places you loved to the man you loved. 'And will you be going to England?' she asked quickly as Thane turned to look at her.

'Definitely. We'll be going there first for at least a couple of weeks.'

'Then perhaps you'll have time to visit us.' She smiled a little mischievously. 'We're on the way to Stratford-on-Avon.'

Thane laughed, immediately catching on. 'We can do Shakespeare and you in one day, huh?'

It was impossible to avoid looking into his eyes then, to see them smiling at her in complete accord. Guiltily she turned away and began to suggest going inside again, but Thane put a hand on her elbow and said, 'How would you like to see the Cloisters? They're only a short walk from here.'

'The Cloisters?'

'They're part of a real French monastery. Randolph Hearst brought them over to America and then they were brought and re-erected here by the man who built the Ocean Club.' He raised his arm to point up the flights of steps. 'You reach them from the top terrace.'

Very aware of the warmth of his hand on her arm, Skye shook her head. 'Hey, I'm English, remember? The Versailles Gardens and a French cloister is more than I can take in one night.'

Again Thane laughed in genuine amusement. 'Too much culture, is that it?'

'Definitely. And also too many steps.'

She firmly turned to go in then, and Thane fell into step beside her. 'But I'd like you to see the Cloisters. If there's time over the weekend, I'll drive you up there so you can reach it from the road.'

'And just where are you two planning to go?' Jodi came walking up the path to meet them with Scott beside her. 'Don't tell me you're trying to steal my fiancé away,' she added teasingly, and went up to take Thane's arm, completely sure that she had voiced an impossibility, so completely confident of his love for her.

Thane grinned. 'Maybe I'll beg Skye to steal me away if this honeymoon trip gets any longer.'

'Is that what you were talking about?' Jodi asked, looking round Thane at Skye.

'Yes. I said that you must come and visit us.'

'Oh, I intend to. I mean to show Thane off to everyone I know in England.'

'How many do you know?' he asked her.

'Oh, thousands,' Jodi answered loftily.

'In that case...' Thane let go of her arm. 'The wedding is definitely off,' he joked.

Jodi laughed delightedly and grabbed his arm back. 'You're too late. Mother's ordered the wedding cake.'

Thane sighed theatrically. 'Well, in that case I guess I'll just have to go through with it.'

They walked back to the club, with Thane teasing Jodi some more and Scott joining in, first on one side and then on the other. They obviously were all three used to going around together, making Skye

feel like the outsider she was. But it was Thane,
not Scott, who brought her back into the conversation, who let the others go ahead and walked
along beside her.

The two men teased Jodi quite a lot, Skye noticed during the weekend. But it was mostly because her cousin deliberately provoked it, making
some remark that would leave her wide open, and
loving it when they immediately picked her up, even
though she pretended to pout and be angry. If anything, it was Scott who probably teased her the most
and looked as if he enjoyed it more. Watching them
when they all went out on the motor-cruiser the next
day, Skye felt that Thane teased Jodi almost automatically, rather as an adult would to indulge a
child.

The original idea of the trip on the motor-boat
was to sail to the island of Grand Bahama and visit
the town of Freeport. They set out early, before the
sun got too hot, the men in T-shirts and shorts,
Aunt Helen in a summer dress and the two girls in
shorts and suntops over their swimsuits. It was quite
a large boat, but sleek and fast with a raised flying
bridge from where Uncle John or one of his local
crewmen steered the vessel. At deck level there was
a large saloon with a bar that contained every kind
of drink Skye had ever heard of and a whole lot
more that she hadn't, and below decks there were
several luxurious cabins, a galley, dining-room and
quarters for the crew.

Skye sat down on the open deck with the others
as they ate a late breakfast served to them by the
efficient, smiling steward. Everyone was relaxed and
in a happy mood. There was a breeze over the sea,

but the water was quite calm even when they headed out over the reefs to the open sea. As they sailed further out, the colour of the sea changed from shades of turquoise to a deep cobalt blue, a rich colour that Skye had only seen before in old stained-glass church windows when the sun shone through them and made that vivid blue come alive.

As New Providence receded to sit low on the horizon, the men brought out fishing-rods which they attached to holders in the stern of the boat near a chair that was bolted to the deck.

The fish didn't seem to be biting and the lines were left to look after themselves. Loungers were brought out and Jodi and Aunt Helen stripped down to their bikinis to sunbathe, while the men took off their T-shirts. With little hesitation, Skye did the same, but she was wearing a one-piece bathing-suit, in a soft deep pink material that crossed and gathered into figure-hugging folds, although it was cut quite high at the legs.

'Your skin is so white!' Jodi exclaimed. 'You should have had some sun-lamp treatment before you came out.' She ran a hand along the length of her own deeply tanned legs, looking at them complacently. Skye looked to see if Thane was watching, but he was standing in the stern with Uncle John, looking out over the sea. Instead it was Scott who was watching Jodi, an appreciative curve to his lips. Jodi let her fingers follow the line of her bikini and met Scott's eyes with a provocative pout, almost as if she had known he would be watching her.

'You must be careful you don't burn,' Aunt Helen warned Skye. 'The sun is very intense, you know.'

'I will.' Skye sat on the lounger next to Jodi and waited until Scott had joined the other men before saying, 'How long have you and Thane been engaged?'

'Only a couple of months.' She saw Skye's surprised look and gave a shrug and a smile. 'I guess it's what you might call a whirlwind romance. We've only been going out together for a few months, but once we got engaged there didn't seem any point in waiting around to get married.'

'You've only known him for a few months?' Skye tried to speak levelly, to keep the astonishment out of her voice.

'No, I've known him much longer than that. Almost eighteen months, I suppose.' She looked at Skye under her lashes and moved nearer to say confidingly, 'Actually, I used to go out with Scott. That's how I met Thane. But he was dating another girl and we all used to go around in a foursome. That went on for nearly a year, I suppose, although Scott and I weren't all that serious; we mostly only saw each other when I was staying at our apartment in New York. But then Thane split with Carol—that was the girl he was dating—and I happened to go up to New York soon afterwards. Scott was away on a business trip and Thane and I ran into each other and we went out for a meal, and I guess...' She shrugged and smiled again. 'I guess it all went from there.'

'Didn't Scott have anything to say?' Skye asked curiously. She glanced over to where the two younger men were leaning over the rail together, looking out for schools of fish. 'They still seem very friendly.'

'Oh, they are. Well, of course Scott wasn't very happy, to say the least, but he soon realised that Thane and I were in love and obviously he didn't want to lose his closest friend as well as his girl-friend.' Jodi gave a satisfied, gurgling laugh. 'Most of the time we go around in a threesome. Sometimes Mother says she isn't sure which one I'm engaged to. Isn't that silly?'

Skye thought it was strange, to say the least. If she had been engaged to Thane, she wouldn't have wanted another man around all the time—especially an ex-boyfriend! She wondered how close Jodi had been to Scott. If they had been dating for almost a year, then surely they would have exchanged more than kisses? And it seemed very odd that Thane was willing to have Scott around so much, too. But perhaps it was different for men, maybe they weren't so possessive, so jealous. Or maybe it was just that they were Americans, New Yorkers, and they were all far more enlightened and broad-minded than she was. Now Skye came to think of it, there had been some pretty odd set-ups, even in the small-town art college that she had attended. But even so she said, 'Does Scott come down with Thane every weekend?'

'Mostly. Scott got so used to coming down here when we were dating, you see. It would be a shame to take that away from him; he enjoys it so much.'

Skye lay back on her lounger and closed her eyes, realising that Jodi had contradicted herself. First she had said that she mostly only saw Scott in New York, and then she had said he was in the habit of coming down to the Bahamas regularly, which implied a much closer relationship. So which was it?

And why bother to lie, anyway? Unless she was trying to convince herself, to assuage her own guilt feelings, and hadn't quite made it yet.

After half an hour in the sun, Skye moved her lounger into the shade and began to rub some after-sun lotion on to her skin.

'Want any help with that?' Scott strolled across the deck and squatted down beside her. He was wearing just shorts and loafers, his tall, rangy body very tanned, his eyes assessing her behind the dark glasses he wore.

'If you wouldn't mind doing my back for me.' Skye handed him the bottle of lotion, and he poured some on to his hand as Skye turned to sit with her back to him.

The lotion felt very cool against her hot skin. Scott used both hands, rubbing rhythmically across her shoulders and down her back. His hands were firm and felt almost sensuous, but they didn't give Skye the lift he intended her to feel. They were just the wrong hands, that was all. And anyway, Scott had only been working on Skye's back for a minute or so when Jodi said impatiently, 'You're putting far too much on. Here, let me.' And she came and pushed Scott aside. 'You're getting white strap marks with that suit,' Jodi pointed out sharply. 'Why don't you wear a bikini like everyone else?' She rubbed in the moisturiser, her long nails leaving marks on Skye's back. 'There, that's better.'

'Thanks.' Skye stood up, and as she did so saw Thane watching them, his mouth a little grim. And he had reason to be; it must have been more than obvious that Jodi hadn't wanted Scott to be attentive to anyone other than herself.

Jodi must have seen Thane's face at the same time. She ran to stand beside him at the stern, putting her arms round his waist and leaning against him, smiling up into his eyes. Thane, too, was only wearing shorts. Jodi began to stroke his back, much more gently than she had Skye's, and to brush her legs, then her body, against Thane's, her hips rotating voluptuously. With a sudden movement, Thane put his arm round her and pulled her against him, kissing her hungrily. Skye looked quickly away, feeling like a voyeur. But Scott had no such qualms; he was watching them openly, his mouth twisted, his jaw set into a rigid line.

Skye went into the saloon, feeling as if she had a bad taste in her mouth. Her aunt and uncle were in there, reading the papers, and she said, 'Hello, any chance of a drink?'

'Of course. What would you like?' Uncle John got up and went behind the bar.

'Something long, cool and exotic, please.'

'Someone's talking about me again.' Thane came in behind her and sat down at the bar stool next to hers. 'Or maybe it describes you better,' he corrected himself.

Skye wrinkled her nose. 'Is it possible for a person to be both cool and exotic?'

He let his eyes run over her for a second, then nodded. 'Oh, I think so.'

'Here we are; one Barracuda coming up.'

Uncle John handed her a cocktail in a tall glass and Skye turned to thank him. She wondered why Thane had left Jodi so quickly after that rough embrace. He didn't seem at all angry, but she noticed that his mouth hadn't entirely lost that grim look it had had earlier. Looking through the windows she saw that Jodi was lying on her lounger again, apparently reading a book, but there was no sign of Scott.

They began to talk about fishing, and presently Uncle John took her to the stern and showed her the various lines and told her what kind of fish they were hoping to catch. Thane came along too and stood beside them, listening.

'Here, sit in that fighting chair and see what it feels like,' her uncle encouraged her. 'There's this shoulder harness you have to strap on,' he told her as Skye obeyed him. 'That's so that the fish doesn't pull you overboard.'

'Are they that big?' Skye said in astonishment.

'Are they big?' Thane echoed. 'Why, it's even been known that a blue whale could be caught on one of these...' His voice faded as he looked into Skye's face, then he shook his head. 'No, sorry. They're large, but they're not that big.'

'Sometimes you can go the whole day without catching anything at all,' her uncle began, but, almost to belie his words, suddenly a ratchet began to scream and one of the rods bent double as a fish caught on the line began to speed away.

'It's taken the bait!' Uncle John shouted, and grabbed the line. 'Quick, Thane, get in the chair.'

'Sorry, Skye.'

Thane lifted her bodily out of the chair and set her down on the deck, then jumped into the seat and pulled on the harness as the rod was jammed into the holder in front of the fighting chair. The boat had throttled back and was lying dead in the water, but the line continued to scream out, the noise jarring the senses. Scott and a crewman came running up and someone threw a bucket of water over the line as it began to smoke. Then, mercifully, they clicked off the ratchet and the line went singing out until at last it stopped.

'Must be half a mile at least,' Scott said excitedly. 'I wonder what it is—tuna or marlin.'

'It's big, whatever it is. OK, Thane, try pulling him in.' But Thane had already braced his legs against the transom and was beginning to pull in the line.

Skye thought that she would never forget that fight between man and fish. It was a long, exhausting battle. Thane's muscles tensed and bulged as he slowly wound the fish in, foot by foot, only to have the fish suddenly take off again so that the last ten minutes' work was lost in as many seconds and the fight began again for every inch of line. His forehead was wet with perspiration, the sinews in his legs and arms stood out, and his smooth skin gleamed beneath the heat of the sun. It seemed impossible for him to go on fighting, but from somewhere Thane found the strength and, about an hour after the first strike, there was a shout from the bridge and Skye followed the pointing hands to see a big, metallic blue fish with a nose as sharp and long as a spear suddenly leap out of the water behind them. For a moment it seemed to hang in the air, curved and infinitely graceful, the sun radiating off its wet skin and turning it to bright steel. Skye caught her breath, overwhelmed by its beauty.

'A marlin!' Scott shouted. 'It must weigh well over two hundred pounds.'

This time, as if seeing the boat had told him his fate, the marlin dived very deep. Thane began to pull again and crank the line, slowly gaining on the angry, frightened fish as it fought for its life. Again there was a shout from the bridge that they could see the shadow of the fish near the surface now. His breath rasping in his dry throat, Thane made a last supreme effort to pull the marlin into the side where the crewmen were waiting to kill it and haul it aboard. Skye thought of that beautiful, graceful creature that had put up such a long and gallant fight for its life, and couldn't bear to think of it lying torn and bleeding on the deck. Going quickly up to Thane, she touched him on the shoulder and said fiercely, 'Let it go now. *Please* let it go.'

He turned and blinked at her, his chest heaving, his throat gasping for breath. For a moment he seemed too exhausted to understand, but then his eyes met hers, very blue, very intense. Their gaze held for a long moment and then he gave the briefest of nods before turning. 'Cut the line,' he rasped.

Scott turned to him in angry astonishment. 'No, bring it aboard.'

'You heard me! Cut it.'

The other men looked at one another, plainly caught up in the excitement of the chase, but then Uncle John nodded and a crewman reached over the side to cut the line close to the fish. Running to the side, Skye looked down and saw the great, spent creature, just a few feet below, roll almost listlessly in the water, then feel its freedom and find the last dregs of strength to dive down, down and away. Skye turned exultantly and found Thane standing and watching beside her. 'Oh, thank you. Thank you!' she exclaimed and, too choked with emotion to think, she reached out to hug him in gratitude.

Thane put his hands on her shoulders, his eyes intent on her face, but suddenly Skye realised that they were all watching her. Flushing scarlet, she pulled out of his hold, muttered an apology, and turned to run across the deck to the obscurity of the saloon.

CHAPTER THREE

THERE were too many windows in the big saloon. Skye went down below to one of the sleeping cabins where she'd left her things, and changed back into her shorts and a shirt. She had a nasty suspicion that she had made a complete fool of herself back there and that Jodi would be angry. But she had been so afraid that they would kill the fish, and Thane was the only one who had the power to let it go free. Even though he had been the one to defeat the marlin and had the right to claim it as his prize, Skye had somehow known that he was the only man who had enough generosity of heart to let it go. That, and a respect for the opponent who had given him such a marvellous fight. And her reaction had been completely natural; she would have been grateful to anyone in the same circumstances. But would she have been quite so quick to hug anyone else? Her uncle, say? Or Scott? Skye hoped that she would; hoped anyway that she would have been equally grateful.

She was brushing her hair when her aunt came to find her. 'Are you all right, Skye?'

'Yes, fine. I'm—er—I'm sorry about what happened.'

'There's no need to be. I suppose I should have guessed that you'd be anti big-game fishing. I know your parents always disapproved of hunting and that kind of thing.'

And so it was glossed over. Skye had to put up with a little teasing from her uncle when she came up on deck, but no one seemed to think anything of her hugging Thane, not even Jodi, who only laughed and said, 'Scott's made me promise to lock you in the cabin when it's his turn to play a fish. He says that there's no way he would let it go.'

And Thane? He had gone to shower and came up after Skye did. He, too, came in for some ragging, but he looked across at her and gave a quick smile of understanding that made Skye feel warm inside.

They had lunch in the boat and shortly afterwards reached Grand Bahama. Here, in Freeport, there was an international bazaar built in the architectural styles of many different countries, with all of the shops and restaurants supposed to be selling the merchandise and food of their own nations. It was an unique idea, and ordinarily Skye would have enjoyed exploring the bazaar. She did enjoy it at first, but it was very hot and she soon began to feel tired. Her aunt and Jodi were enthusiastically looking for clothes and things that they couldn't get in Nassau. Skye tried to keep up, but found her legs starting to ache and knew that she would have to stop and rest.

It was Thane who came to her rescue. He stopped and said, 'I'm beat. I'm going to find a place to have a drink.' He turned to Jodi. 'How about you?' But Jodi wanted to do some more shopping, so he looked at Skye. 'Would you like a drink with me?'

She nodded gratefully. 'Please.'

Uncle John had stayed on the boat—to have a siesta, Skye suspected—but Scott went on with Jodi and Aunt Helen while Thane and Skye found Michel's, a sidewalk café in the French quarter that immediately made Skye feel as if she was in Paris. All it needed was artists painting at their easels and you could almost believe you were in Montmartre. She said as much to Thane, and added, 'I suppose that's another place you'll be visiting when you and Jodi go to Europe?'

'I guess so.' He sat back in his chair, relaxed now, his long, bare legs stretched out in front of him and crossed at the ankles.

Skye wondered why she'd said that to him; she hadn't thought before that she had a masochistic nature. Awkwardly she said, 'I wanted to thank you for letting the marlin go free. It was very *kind* of you.'

Thane turned his head to look at her, then reached up to take off his sunglasses and leant forward to put his elbows on the table between them, his eyes on her face. 'I don't think anyone has ever told me I was kind before—not someone who meant it.'

'Don't people say that very much in America?'

'Oh, sure—but it's usually just a politeness.' Skye looked down at the table, her heart beating faster than it should, but her head came up again quickly when Thane said, 'I would have let the marlin go anyway.'

'You would?'

'A lot of people do, though some of them tag the fish first just to prove they've caught it.'

'But you didn't do that.'

He shook his head. 'I fought him and I won. I know it, so what does it matter whether anyone else does? And I've seen too many sports fishing-boats come in full of men laughing and bragging about their catch. They hoist the fish up by their tails to a metal crossbar and have their pictures taken with the catch. Then they go off to a bar to celebrate and just leave the fish hanging there.'

'Don't they take them home? Have them mounted or something like that?'

'No, they're too big. At night the local fishermen come and cut them down. Then they just chop them up and use them as bait for sharks. So, anything that's no good to eat, I throw back.'

'Does Scott do that? And Uncle John?'

Thane's lips thinned a little. 'That's up to them.'

Their drinks came and they sat in silence for a while, but it wasn't an unpleasant silence, Skye didn't feel that she *had* to find something to talk about. She just enjoyed sitting in the shade, drinking the cool Coke, knowing that soon Thane would talk to her again and that she would be in-tensely interested in all he had to say.

He didn't disappoint her. Putting down his drink, he said, 'There's a better way to capture fish.' And, when she raised her eyebrows, he said, 'On film. With an underwater camera. Do you swim?'

'Why, yes, but . . .'

'Then you must go down to the coral reefs. The water is so clear that you can see for yards all around you. And the depth varies from around ten feet to a hundred. But perhaps the best time to go is at night, with a dive light; then you see the true colours of the fish and the coral.'

'Why can't you see them by day?' Skye queried in fascination.

'Because with natural light you're diving in a kind
of blue twilight. The colours gradually disappear
one by one as you go deeper. Red goes first, so that
if you cut yourself your blood looks green. Not that
it's a good idea to cut yourself in these seas because
of sharks.'

'Don't fish sleep at night?'

'Some do, which lets you get real close. You can
even touch them. But most of the fish come alive
at night. And they're real noisy. They grunt and
groan and click; the sea's full of noise.'

Skye laughed delightedly. 'It sounds wonderful.
I wish I could see it.'

'So we'll go down. How about tomorrow?'

The temptation to be alone with him again, to
let him show her the undersea world was very great,
but Skye slowly shook her head. 'Thanks, but I
was told not to swim for a while yet. And I'm not
very experienced at diving; I've only been down a
few times with my brother.'

'That's a pity. When do you think you'll be able
to swim again?'

'Perhaps in a couple of weeks.'

They talked of other things and Skye found him
very knowledgeable, with interest in a wide range
of subjects. But he didn't hog the conversation; he
was more than willing to listen to her, to her
opinions, often asking her what she thought about
different topics. And he had a sense of humour too,
often laughing at something she said or making her
laugh with him. And because he was such an appreciative listener Skye sparkled in his company,
losing her usual initial reserve and able to tell him

amusing anecdotes with a pithy, quiet wit that he seemed to enjoy.

In his company the time seemed to fly by, and Skye was amazed to find that over an hour had passed when the others came back to join them. She felt a twinge of disappointment when she saw them come into sight, but hastily swallowed it and greeted Jodi with a smile. 'You look as if you've bought up half the bazaar with all those parcels.'

'I bought a most gorgeous hand-crocheted bikini,' Jodi enthused. 'And a couple of mohair sweaters.'

'Well, I imagine the sweaters will be useful in England,' Skye commented, 'but somehow I don't think it will ever be hot enough there for a bikini.'

Jodi laughed and took a parcel from her shopping bag, unwrapping it to hold up the two pieces of a bright yellow bikini, so intricately worked that they almost looked like lace. She gave Thane a provocative look under her lashes. 'Well, what do you think?'

His lips twitched. 'What there is of it would appear to do its job,' he answered, being deliberately enigmatic.

An indignant frown puckered Jodi's brow, but Scott said quickly, 'He means that it turns him on. Don't worry. He likes it.'

Jodi looked from one to the other of them, for once not sure if they were teasing her, but obviously deciding to accept that they were because she smiled at Thane and said, 'Perhaps I should have waited until we were alone before I showed it to you.'

The sexual connotations were there in her voice, heavy with meaning. Skye looked away, remembering the kiss they had exchanged on the boat. She was sure now that they must be lovers. And what about Scott? If he had also been Jodi's lover, how must he feel now, to have Jodi's relationship with Thane flaunted in his face? Skye just couldn't understand how Jodi could be so cruel, but then glanced up and caught a gleam of almost coy amusement in her cousin's eyes and realised that she was enjoying the situation. Was that why she tolerated—no, *encouraged*—Scott to still come to visit her with Thane, because it gave her a thrill to make them jealous?

They had another drink while Aunt Helen showed her some exquisitely embroidered table linen that she'd bought in the Chinese section of the bazaar and which was to be part of Jodi's wedding present. Seeing it made Skye remember that she hadn't yet bought a present. Her mother, if she came out for the wedding, had promised to bring a family present of Wedgwood china, but Skye felt that as a bridesmaid she ought to give Jodi something herself. She mentioned as much to Aunt Helen when they were walking back to the boat, and asked her if Jodi had a wedding-present list.

'Well, no. Most of the people we mix with here are American, and it's their custom for the bridesmaids and the girlfriends of the bride to give her a bridal shower just before the wedding. Usually they choose what they want to give themselves.'

'Have you any idea what Jodi needs?'

Her aunt looked slightly embarrassed. 'To be honest, Skye, I don't think she really *needs* anything. You know they're going to buy a bigger apartment in New York, and maybe they'll be short of something then, but until they do they're going to live in Thane's apartment and that's already fully equipped. Tell you what, why don't you ask Jodi yourself?'

Skye did so, the first opportunity she had to get Jodi on her own, which wasn't until they were back at the house in Nassau much later that evening. They had had dinner on the boat and then put on cassette music and danced out on the deck as they sailed back to New Providence. Skye had one very slow dance with her uncle and a slightly faster number with Scott, but then sat down on one of the loungers, content to watch the swaying figures silhouetted against the sunset. As soon as they got back to the house Jodi wanted to change and go on to a nightclub, even though it was almost ten o'clock, but Skye said firmly that she had had enough for one day. Her uncle agreed with her and said, 'And it wouldn't hurt you to stay at home yourself, Jodi. You must remember that Skye has been ill. And she is your guest.'

'Oh, please,' Skye interrupted in embarrassment, 'no one has to stay at home because of me. All of you go. I'll be fine here by myself.'

'You see,' Jodi joined in. 'Skye wants to go to bed, so what's the point of us staying in? I'm not tired, and I'm sure Thane and Scott aren't. Are you?' she appealed, turning to look at them. 'Why, we've hardly done anything all day.'

Scott glanced at Thane, then shrugged and said, 'Well, I'm quite willing to go out if that's what Jodi wants, but of course I'm equally willing to stay in if that's what you think we ought to do, sir,' he added, addressing Uncle John.

Jodi gave one her most winning pouts and went over to her father, sliding her arm round his neck and kissing him on the cheek. 'Come on, Daddy. You know how you enjoy going to the casino and playing roulette. Maybe you'll win again like you did last time. Please. Mmm? Please let's go.'

She tickled his neck and Uncle John had to relax his stern expression and laugh. 'All right, young lady. You know I can't say no to you, don't you?' He smiled indulgently, but then frowned. 'But I don't like leaving Skye here alone.'

'She'll hardly be alone,' Jodi protested. 'The housekeeper and her husband will be sleeping in the house. And anyway, you don't mind leaving me here alone when you go out.'

'That's true.' He turned to Skye. 'If you're sure you don't mind?'

'I've already said I'll be OK. Please, it's nice of you to worry, but I'll be fine.'

So they all went up to change, and Skye followed Jodi to her room and tapped on her door about twenty minutes later.

'Come on in.'

Skye went inside and saw Jodi just putting on her bra in front of the floor-length mirror. She turned her head, quite unconcerned about who it might be. 'Oh, it's you. Changed your mind about coming along?'

Skye shook her head. 'No. From what I've heard, casinos tend to stay open very late and I already feel tired. I'd be falling asleep in the nearest chair.'

Jodi nodded. 'I knew you wouldn't want to spoil everyone else's fun, that's why I persuaded Pop to go.' As she spoke, Jodi took a beautiful dress in shades of blue from her walk-in wardrobe and slipped it over her head.

'What a gorgeous dress. Did you buy it here?'

'No, in New York. I buy most of my clothes there.'

Talking about buying things made Skye remember why she'd come, so she said, 'Mother is buying you some china as a wedding present, but I'd like to get you something, too. Have you any idea what you'd like?'

Leaning towards the mirror, Jodi put on a thick layer of pearly pink lipstick. 'Not really. I'll think about it, OK?' She sprayed herself liberally with scent and then sorted out an evening bag from one of the shelves of a cupboard that was crammed full of bags.

Skye got up to have a look inside Jodi's wardrobes and exclaimed, 'My word, Jodi, you've got enough clothes to start a department store, let alone a shop!'

'Oh, these are only my casual clothes,' Jodi laughed. 'You should see the outfits I keep in New York. I'd better go, the others will be waiting. See you.'

'Bye.' But she had already run out of the room. Going along the gallery to her own room, Skye crossed to the balcony and waved as they all got into the car. Watching them go, she reflected on how easily Jodi had got her own way, and the wiles she had used to do it. A grin creased Skye's mouth as she thought of her own father's horror if she had used such tactics on him. She could imagine the way he would have cringed and demanded to know if she was ill or something. He had treated his children as fellow adults from the moment they had left school, and his faith in them had been fully justified: neither of them had ever resorted to childish pranks or behaviour again. And their mother, of course, had very seldom treated them as children ever since they had been able to walk and talk.

A leisurely bath was called for, Skye decided, and she lay back in the hot water, not yet used to the novelty of a jacuzzi. The only thing was, it tended to make the pages of the book she was reading rather wet. Putting the book aside, Skye closed her eyes. She would stay home and do some painting tomorrow, she decided. What with one thing and another, she had hardly done any work since she'd arrived in Nassau. And maybe it would be wise to stay home because, although she had enjoyed today, the highlight of it had been that hour she had spent alone with Thane. Which wouldn't do at all. She was much too attracted to him, she realised. Which was crazy when she had only known him for such a short time, and especially when she knew that he was shortly to be married. And to her own cousin, at that. She tried to push him out of her mind, but he kept returning; she could picture his strong, handsome face and that chin with the cleft in it that should have detracted from his good looks but which somehow fascinated her.

Angry with herself, Skye got out of the bath and towelled herself dry. Her appendix scar was small and neat and almost completely healed now. Remembering what Jodi had said about a bikini, she wondered whether the scar would show and walked through into the bedroom to look into the mirror there. She had left only a bedside lamp burning, and she lifted her hand to switch on the main light. But her hand froze as she saw a figure go past the uncurtained window! For a moment terror filled her and Skye couldn't think, but then thoughts came all too quickly. She didn't know where the housekeeper and her husband slept, or if they would hear her if she called out. There was no phone in her bedroom, and even if there was she didn't know the emergency number here to ring for help. Pulling her bathrobe tighter around her, Skye quietly crossed the room and tried the french windows. They were unlocked. A quick glance round the room showed her that nothing seemed to have been disturbed, but then she had nothing very much to steal. However, there might easily be jewellery lying about in Jodi's or her aunt's rooms.

Slipping quickly out on to the balcony, Skye looked along it, but could see no one. She moved to the rail and looked down into the garden, but there were too many shrubs giving deep shadows in which an intruder could easily hide. She hesitated, wondering what to do, then heard a creaking sound as somebody moved along the balcony behind her! Gasping with fright, Skye spun around. 'Who—who's there?' she stammered.

'Skye? It's OK. It's me, Thane.'

'Oh!' Skye gave a great shudder of relief and clung to one of the uprights, her legs feeling suddenly weak.

'Are you all right?' Thane came quickly to her side and put a supportive hand under her elbow.

'You frightened the life out of me. I thought you were a burglar.'

'You'd better come inside and sit down.' Taking her back into her room, Thane sat her down on the bed and looked at her anxiously. 'You're not going to faint or anything?'

'What? No, of course not.' Skye tried to pull herself together and saw that he was wearing only a pair of bathing trunks, the wet material hugging his lower body. 'You're all wet.'

'I've been swimming.' He put a hand on her shoulder. 'I'm sorry if I scared you. I . . .'

'I didn't know you were here. Why didn't you . . .?'

They both spoke at the same time and stopped together. Thane smiled and gestured. 'Go ahead.'

'I thought you went with the others.' Skye felt the pressure of his hand on her shoulder, and wondered if he could feel the beat of her heart as much as she could.

'I changed my mind. Decided to come back for a swim.'

'Then it was you I saw go past my room?'

He nodded. 'I came up the outside stairs and along the balcony so as not to drip water through the house. We usually do. I'm sorry I scared you. I thought you must have gone to sleep with the light on.'

'No, I was in the bath.' Suddenly aware that she had nothing on under the robe, so that quite a long expanse of bare leg was showing, Skye stood up rather abruptly.

Thane didn't move away. His hand was still on her shoulder in a comforting gesture and he was very close. The anxiety had gone from his eyes, but he said again, 'Are you sure you're OK? Is there anything I can get you?'

'No, thank you. You must think I'm an idiot, especially after I said that I'd be all right alone,' Skye remarked ruefully.

His eyebrows lifting in surprise, Thane said, 'On the contrary, I think you were very brave to go out there at all if you thought there was a hoodlum around.' He grinned suddenly. 'Brave, but crazy.'

'I was afraid it was a burglar and they might be ransacking Jodi's or Aunt Helen's room,' Skye explained. 'So naturally I had to do something.'

Thane shook his head. 'Facing up to intruders doesn't come naturally to anyone in America, especially women who think they're alone in the house. Do me a favour, will you? Don't ever try it again.'

'So what should I do?'

'Just bolt yourself in the bathroom and let them get on with it.'

Skye looked indignant. 'That sounds very cowardly.'

'Better to be a live coward than a beaten-up heroine.'

He spoke on a flippant note, but when Skye looked into his blue eyes she saw that he was serious, his brows drawn into a frown. She nodded. 'All right, I'll remember.'

Thane looked down at her, seeing the cloud of dark hair about her head, the long, dark lashes under level brows, and the smoothness of her pale skin. 'Everything about you is soft,' he said wonderingly. 'Soft and gentle. And yet you have such courage. I don't know any other woman who would have gone out alone to face an intruder.'

Her heart was beating painfully, but Skye managed to laugh and say, 'It wasn't courage at all; it was only anger because I thought someone might be stealing Jodi's jewellery.' She looked directly into Thane's eyes. 'And after all, Jodi is my hostess as well as my cousin. And she has been very kind to me.'

The mention of Jodi's name brought them both back to reality. Stepping back, Thane took his hand from her shoulder and said, 'Perhaps it might be an idea if I check all the windows before I turn in. You sure you're OK now?' And, when Skye nodded, 'I'll say goodnight, then. See you tomorrow. Oh, and you'd better lock these windows after me. You'll sleep better that way.'

He went out on to the balcony and waited until Skye had closed and locked the windows, then lifted his hand in farewell and went on towards his own room, his almost naked figure silvered by the moonlight. Skye watched him go and then slowly drew the curtains together. She stood still for a long moment, feeling the irregular beating of her heart, letting it gradually subside into something approaching normality before she turned away and finished getting ready for bed. But now she was fully awake and lay in the darkness, making no attempt not to think about Thane.

Why had he come back? she wondered. Not that it mattered. She knew now, had probably known all along, that what she felt for him was more than attraction. When he had put his hand on her shoulder she had wanted to go to him, to be held close in his arms. For comfort, yes, but more than that. Such a strong physical attraction was new to Skye, and she wouldn't have known how to handle it with any man. But, strangely enough, with Thane it didn't represent any problems, because she didn't have to deal with it, she just had to deny it completely. And try to hide it, of course. And the only way Skye could think of to do that was by avoiding Thane as much as she possibly could. Certainly she must take care never to be alone with him again. For her own sake as much as anything else. It was going to be very hard, Skye realised, to hide her feelings, and even harder to deny herself the pleasure of seeing Thane and being with him, but it had to be done. Whatever effort it cost her, Jodi must never find out.

It might not be too difficult to distance herself from Thane, she decided unhappily. If he only came to Nassau at the weekends, she could plead tiredness so that she didn't have to go out with the others. Or, better still, perhaps she could make a point of being nicer to Scott so that she could suggest they went out alone and left Thane and Jodi by themselves. Somehow she couldn't see Jodi jumping at the idea, but if Thane was in love with Jodi surely he would . . . *If* Thane was in love with Jodi? What had put that idea in her head? Of course he was in love with her. He was going to marry her, wasn't he? It was merely wishful thinking, Skye realised.

An impossible dream that would never come true. It was just her bad luck that she'd fallen for a man who wasn't free. It must happen to thousands of women, she supposed. And to men, of course, which was probably why there were so many broken marriages in the world. Just because a person was married it didn't mean that some sort of biological process took place and they were no longer attractive to the opposite sex. Skye sighed and turned her face into the pillow, knowing that she ought really to find some excuse and go home to England, putting Thane out of her heart and mind forever, but not having the strength to do it.

Skye didn't have to plead tiredness the next morning; there were dusky shadows around her eyes for all to see. Her aunt immediately told her that she must rest, and would have made her lie on a lounger all day, but Skye insisted that she would be able to relax far more if she was allowed to paint. Aunt Helen obviously thought that painting didn't come under the category of work, so after breakfast Skye established herself in the shade of a tree with her easel in front of her while the others went to play tennis and have lunch at the house of a friend in the luxury estate of Lyford Cay at the western end of the island.

It was good to lose herself in the creative process she loved. She had intended to do some work, but weakly let herself be bewitched by the rich West Indian light and vivid colours, and instead painted the view from the garden looking out over the sea. There was so much colour there—not the soft greens and pale blues of the English countryside and sky that she was used to, but bright, strong colours that were a delight to mix and brush on.

She had hardly spoken to Thane that morning, only to say hello as she had to the others. And Jodi had hardly spoken to him at breakfast, either. Skye had come down rather late, but gathered from Jodi's frosty face that she was annoyed with Thane for having come back early last night. In contrast, Jodi was especially nice to Scott, laughing and joking with him and letting Thane see that he was in the doghouse. Skye looked at Thane to see how he was taking it, but he seemed quite calm and relaxed, almost as if he was immune to Jodi's treatment, which of course made her madder than ever. But once Skye saw his eyes narrowing as he watched Jodi put a familiar hand on Scott's arm, and she knew that he wouldn't for long tolerate such a situation. A small shiver ran up Skye's spine and she looked away, feeling embarrassed, especially as it transpired that it was because of her that Thane had come back.

Turning to Skye, Jodi said, 'You *were* all right last night, weren't you?'

'Why, yes, I suppose so. Although I . . .'

But before she'd finished Jodi interrupted to say, 'I knew you would be. We happened to pass the servants walking down the road when we were going out last night, and Thane insisted on going back to the house. Of course I told him you'd be OK by yourself, but he wouldn't believe me.'

'Oh.' She nodded at Thane. 'Thanks.'

'I was tired myself,' he said dismissively, and stood up, a frown in his eyes. 'Guess I'll go and change.'

Skye hadn't seen him again because he'd gone straight out to the car without coming back into the garden, but the fact that he'd cared enough to not let her be alone in an empty house left a warm glow in her heart.

Her brush stilled several times as Skye thought of it, and it took quite an effort of will to persuade herself that Thane would have done the same for anyone; it was innate good manners that had brought him back and not any feelings for her. At lunchtime Skye took a break to eat a crisp salad that the smiling housekeeper brought for her, and then fell asleep for over an hour when she had only lain on the lounger for an intended five minutes' rest. She was cross with herself when she woke, for the sun had gone down and the light had changed. It meant that she would have to wait until tomorrow to finish the picture, although there was still quite a lot of detail she could put in today.

She was filling in the brilliant red blossoms of a tree when the others came back at about three o'clock. They came up behind her to see the painting and were flatteringly enthusiastic. 'Hey, that's great!' Jodi, the first to look, exclaimed. 'I'd no idea you were so talented. Pop, come and look at Skye's picture.'

Her aunt and uncle came over and were equally complimentary. 'Would you let me commission you to do another one for me?' Uncle John asked. 'It would be marvellous to hang in my office in New York. I'd be able to look at it in the depths of winter and remember that life isn't all snow and ice.'

Skye smiled. 'You can have this one, if you'd like it. It isn't finished yet, though. I'll have to work on it tomorrow.'

'I would, indeed,' he said at once. 'Thank you. You have a rare talent, Skye. That picture is vibrant with life.'

Scott came to add his praise, but Thane had gone inside to shower first and didn't come out to the garden until the others had gone inside. He came down the stairs that led directly from the balcony to the terrace, and stood for a moment looking across at Skye. She had her back to him and was leaning forward, totally absorbed in finishing a tree before she packed up for the day. Crossing the grass, Thane ducked under the branch of the tree she was sitting under and leant a hand against its trunk as he looked over her shoulder at the painting. He had made hardly any noise as he approached, but Skye knew he was there. He stood looking his fill for several minutes, then quoted softly,

'Look from your door, and tell me now
The colour of the sea.
Where can I buy that wondrous dye
And take it home with me?'

Skye turned her head to look at him, immediately intrigued. 'Who wrote that? I don't think I've ever heard it before.'

Moving to lean against the tree trunk, his hands thrust into the pockets of his trousers, Thane said, 'It was a man called Bliss Carman.'

She looked at him suspiciously. 'Are you kidding me? It sounds more like a pop group.'

'No. He was a nineteenth-century poet who came
here and fell in love with the place. And he must
have had an eye for colour, too, to have written
that. But if he'd seen your painting first he would
have had no need to write his poem; he could have
bought your picture and taken the "wondrous dye"
home with him. You're good, Skye.'

She shook her head. 'I'm never going to be a
great artist.' She held up a hand as he went to speak.
'I'm not just being modest. I know that I'm quite
good and that some of my paintings occasionally
get close to being very good. But there's nothing
fantastic about them. I don't have the originality
or brilliance to be outstanding.'

'And does that make you unhappy?'

Skye raised her head, pondering the question.
The sun was lower in the sky now and was shining
through the foliage of the tree, sending shafts that
dappled Thane in its light and shade. I would be
happy if I could paint him as he looks now, she
thought, then somehow wrenched her mind away
and said, 'No, I'm not unhappy. Because I know
my limitations. I learnt those at art college. For a
while, when I realised that I would never be more
than mediocre, I felt like throwing it all up, but
then I realised that I had to make a living and art
was the only thing I was even half-way good at. So
I stayed on and settled for second best.' She paused
for a moment, then said, 'But I have a feeling that
it's not something you'd ever be content with.'

'Second best?' A brooding look came into
Thane's eyes. 'Maybe I already have.'

'Aren't you a good lawyer?' Skye asked
hesitantly.

His mouth twisted into a rueful laugh. 'I wasn't thinking about my work.' He shrugged and lifted an arm over his head to reach a branch of the tree. 'I try to be good at my job, yes.'

'And are you ambitious? Jodi said you were.'

'Did she? Yeah, I guess I am. At the moment that's the way I see my life going. A top lawyer and then into business for myself, maybe even into politics. That's what Jodi wants me to do.'

'And you? Is that what you want for yourself?'

Thane's eyes settled on her, very blue, very intense, as if he could see into her soul. 'Doesn't every man want to get as far as he can in his chosen career?'

Slowly Skye said, 'I suppose it depends on what it costs along the way, and whether what he eventually achieves is worth the effort—worth the sacrifices.'

He didn't question what she meant, he already knew the sacrifices. 'Maybe the rewards are better in America, more worth the fight.'

Skye nodded and looked back at her painting. 'I wish I knew the name of that tree,' she remarked as she added the final touch of colour.

'It's a poinciana. But it's usually called a flamboyant, or flame tree.'

'Flame tree.' Skye smiled. 'I like that. It almost looks as if it's on fire.' She stood up. 'I shall have to finish it tomorrow.' Turning to look at Thane, she added lightly, 'When you're back in New York working your way up the ladder of success.'

He looked at her sharply, catching the wry note in her voice. His lips twisting a little, he said, 'You and Jodi, you're different in every way there is.'

'Yes. Yes, I'm afraid we are.' And, picking up her things, Skye walked ahead of him into the house.

It seemed that Jodi had forgiven Thane; she was back to talking to him and touching him a lot. Skye stood talking to her aunt for a few minutes, and couldn't help but notice because Jodi made it so obvious. Taking her painting gear up to her room, Skye lingered for a little time, almost wishing that she didn't have to go down. But that was not only silly but cowardly. Straightening her shoulders, Skye went downstairs and into the sitting-room, where she stood in the doorway to the terrace for a few moments, watching the others. The three men were sitting at a garden table with drinks in front of them, discussing—or rather, arguing about—some item in the paper, and Jodi and her mother were relaxing on loungers and dissecting the reputation of a woman who had been at the lunch party. It took another effort of will to walk forward and join them, to sit down beside her aunt and accept a drink, to pretend to listen and sympathise with what they were saying. They automatically expected Skye to feel the same way they did about everything, and it never occurred to them that her values might be different. She didn't enjoy this type of conversation, but found it difficult to detach herself from it.

Glancing up, she caught Thane looking at her. He gave a small smile of sympathy, almost as if he guessed her thoughts, though that was impossible, of course. Jodi was speaking at the time, but her tone altered and Skye turned her head to find her cousin watching them. Immediately Jodi jumped up and went over to Thane, standing behind him and putting her arms round him. 'I do wish you didn't have to go back to New York,' she said wistfully, and kissed his neck. 'Everything here is dead without you.' Moving round him, she slid on to Thane's lap, her arms still round his neck. 'Promise you'll phone me every day?'

'I do that already.'

'Then write to me, too, so that I can keep your letters.'

Thane didn't seem particularly embarrassed by Jodi's open display of affection, but he raised an eyebrow and said, 'What brought this on?'

'I just realised how soon you'll be leaving and how much I'll miss you, that's all,' Jodi answered on a defensive note, and she leaned forward to kiss him.

Skye picked up her drink and studied the slice of lemon floating in it. She was beginning to realise that Jodi did this sort of thing on purpose, that there was nothing natural or spontaneous about it at all. It was as if her cousin found it necessary to continually prove to everyone how much she was loved and adored. And perhaps prove it to herself as well? Skye unhesitatingly pushed that errant thought aside. Jodi was kissing Thane ardently, her breasts against his chest, and wriggling her behind, almost as if she wanted to turn him on there and then. But Thane put his hands on her waist and pushed her away, just as Aunt Helen said sharply, 'Jodi, really!'

Jodi just laughed delightedly and ran to sit on her father's lap and kiss him, too. 'I'll miss you, too, so don't be jealous.'

Then she looked across at Scott, who grinned and held out his arms. 'What about me? Won't you miss me, too?'

Jodi laughed again and went to kiss him, lingering on his lap just a little too long. Thane got up and wandered down into the garden, and Jodi immediately followed him, the two moving on through the trees and shrubs until they were out of sight.

After a few moments Scott came to take Jodi's place on the lounger and started to chat to Skye about England, telling her of an exchange visit he'd made there as a student, but his eyes kept returning to the garden. Remembering her resolution to put Thane out of her mind and be nicer to Scott, Skye turned to give him her whole attention, to be bright and friendly, but it was difficult when she, too, was wondering, with not a little self-torture and shame, just how passionately Jodi and Thane were saying goodbye down there in the garden.

The men were leaving at five to catch a plane back to New York, and all three women went to the airport to see them off. There were lots of last-minute hugs and kisses from Jodi and Aunt Helen. Uncle John kissed Skye, too, and told her again how pleased he was that she'd come to stay. Then Scott took her hand and leant forward to kiss her. 'So long, Skye. See you the next time I'm down here.' He kissed her on the lips, not just a peck but something that could have been a proper kiss if Skye hadn't stepped back and smilingly said goodbye.

Then it was Thane's turn. He moved away from Jodi's side and came towards her. Skye firmly held out her hand to shake his, but he merely glanced down at it, gave a small grin, and put a hand on her arm as he bent to kiss her goodbye. But that was too much. At the last moment Skye turned her head a little so that the kiss landed on her cheek. Then her eyes flew to his, wide and vulnerable, before she quickly looked away and said huskily, 'Goodbye, Thane. Have—have a good trip home.'

'Sure.' He studied her for a moment, then went to pick up his hold-all.

And then they were gone, in a flurry of waves and called-out goodbyes. Aunt Helen looked after them and sighed. 'Oh, how I hate this moment. Everything seems so flat for a while when they've gone. Still, this weekend is no different from any other, I suppose.'

She turned to walk back to the car with Jodi beside her, and Skye followed them more slowly, thinking that this weekend had been the most momentous in her life, and that no matter what happened she would never forget it as long as she lived.

CHAPTER FOUR

DURING the next week Skye concentrated as much as she could on her neglected work, but also felt obliged to go out with Jodi and Aunt Helen several times. Having lived on the island for so long, they had lots of friends there and were always being invited out or having people round, and because they were so caught up in the social life of New Providence themselves they thought it was unnatural for Skye to want to stay at home. When she said that she'd like to stay and paint, her aunt became worried that she was feeling ill. So, having been brought up to be a well-trained guest, Skye did as her relations obviously wanted and went along with them.

Jodi was different now the men had gone back; she seemed to relax and be herself, almost as if she had been play-acting at being engaged, at being full of bubbling vitality, during the weekend. Skye had been afraid that Jodi's attitude towards her might have changed, but she was evidently unafraid of any opposition from her when Thane and Scott weren't around, and willingly introduced Skye to all her friends. But every evening she waited eagerly for Thane's phone call, running up immense bills for him as she told him everything she'd been doing, about more wedding presents that had arrived, guests who had accepted invitations, and wedding details that had been finalised.

Listening to Jodi and her aunt discussing the wedding made Skye realise just how close it was. It was planned that in two weeks' time she would go with them to New York to stay in their Manhattan apartment and be fitted for the bridesmaid's dress. Already her measurements had been sent on ahead, so that the dressmaker would only have the last-minute alterations to do. The dresses were to be a pale coral colour with sashes in a darker shade, Jodi told Skye enthusiastically. And she, of course, would be wearing white, but the men were having coral cravats with their morning suits.

'Don't the bride and bridegroom make up their own vows for weddings in America?' Skye asked. 'I saw on a television programme once that they did.' They were sitting by the pool and Skye had a sketch-book on her lap, trying to work out ideas for a series of book illustrations. She had stopped work to listen to Jodi, but now absently turned over a page and began to sketch her cousin.

'But this is going to be a traditional British wedding,' Jodi said firmly. 'In the cathedral here in Nassau, and with the old traditional service. And the reception is being held at the Ocean Club over on Paradise Island. But you know that already.'

'Mm.' Skye's pencil was busy, her eyes flicking to Jodi and back to her sketch-book. 'Are many of Thane's relations coming for the wedding?'

'Quite a few. His parents and sister live in Maryland, but he has people coming from all over the States.' She spoke with satisfaction, evidently enjoying the idea of being the centre of attraction. But then, didn't every bride on her wedding day?

'Tell me about Thane,' Skye invited, willing to undergo even this self-inflicted hurt to learn more about him. 'Have you met his people?'

'Oh, yes. Several times. I met them first when I was seeing Scott. They came up to New York when it was Thane's birthday once, just before Christmas. And we made a party of it and all went out together.'

'All of you?'

'Yes. Scott and I, and Thane's ex-girlfriend, his parents, and his sister Angie and her boyfriend.'

'Is his sister married yet?'

'No. She's not even engaged,' Jodi answered on an unwittingly superior note. 'She broke up with her boyfriend not long after that, I think. She's at college now, taking an advanced degree—the equivalent of our postgraduate courses, I suppose. So I don't have to see her too often, thank goodness.'

Skye looked up. 'You sound as if you don't like her very much.'

Jodi wrinkled her nose. 'I don't. She seems to think that unless you've got a college degree and are holding down a career, you're nothing. She doesn't understand my kind of life-style at all. And his parents aren't much better. His father is a lawyer, too, and his mother is a teacher and still works part-time. Fancy being middle-aged and still working!' Jodi said with a shudder. 'I can't see Mummy doing it.'

'My mother does,' Skye said mildly. 'And she gets a great deal of pleasure from it.'

'But she's a musician,' Jodi protested. 'That's different. That's being creative and—and artistic.'

'And don't you think that teaching can be creative?'

'Well, of course not.' There was indignation in Jodi's voice and Skye knew there was no point in going on; her cousin would never understand the joy that could come when a solitary pupil lit with the inspirational flame of something you had taught.

After that conversation, Skye realised that Jodi and she could never now be close friends, although they had been quite close in childhood. Now they were too different, had been brought up to appreciate entirely diverse life-styles, and could only meet on a social level. It made Skye feel rather sad. She had used to really like Jodi, but now she felt herself growing impatient of her cousin's vanity and weakness. Not that Jodi seemed to have any difficulty in attracting men, Skye thought wryly. But then she remembered that throughout history men had always gone for a pretty face and a good figure rather than brains. So maybe Jodi had it right, after all.

As the week passed there were more and more references to 'what they would do when the men were home'. In this household of women it seemed there were limits to what you could do or where you could go unescorted, even in these enlightened times. And it was the same in many houses on the islands where families had come there to spend the summer, leaving their menfolk to commute from the States every weekend. For Jodi it wasn't so bad, because she knew lots of college-age young men who lived in Nassau that she could go out with, but for Aunt Helen the social functions she attended during the week were predominantly female affairs, so it was no wonder that they looked forward eagerly to the men coming home.

Skye looked forward to it, too, although she knew that she shouldn't. She tried to keep herself busy, finishing her painting of the garden and taking it into Nassau to be framed. She also did some more work on the sketch of Jodi, and one day took her sketch-book down to the harbour and did lots of drawings of the straw market and the busy area around Bay Street. There was so much vitality, so much life going on. She drew the horse-drawn buggies with their fringes and curtains, a man carving weird faces out of pieces of driftwood, a stall full of shells, each intricately lovely in colour and shape, and a native woman surrounded by the piles of richly mouth-watering fruits that she was selling.

But however much time Skye spent on her work, and however often she went out with Jodi and Aunt Helen, the weekend came inexorably nearer and she knew that she was going to have to make up her mind how she was going to behave towards Thane. No, not so much make up her mind, because she knew what she had to do, it was just finding the strength of mind to keep to it. She had to play it cool. To be friendly without being familiar. To somehow deny that instantaneous meeting of minds that had so attracted her. And she must always re-member that Thane was as good as married to her cousin. But most of all she must make absolutely sure that she was never alone with him again. Be-cause she knew that if they were alone for any length of time it would be almost impossible to hide the way she felt about him.

So Skye made a point of not going to the airport to meet him, although it was difficult to avoid this time because Uncle John came home on the Friday evening but Thane and Scott didn't fly down until the Saturday morning. Jodi fully expected Skye to go with her to the airport, but Skye pleaded a headache and stayed in her room until lunchtime. She heard the car arrive and the sound of voices, but this time she didn't go out on to the balcony to look. At lunchtime she couldn't put it off any longer. She changed into a full skirt and pretty matching blouse and went slowly down the stairs.

They were all out at the pool. Skye walked to the edge of the terrace and lifted her hand to shield her eyes from the flashes of light given off by the sun as it reflected on the water. There were more people there than she had expected to see; some friends of Jodi's must have come round and it had turned into a swimming party. Several men were in the pool, their hair darkened by the water so that it was difficult to see who was who. They were playing some kind of team game with a large, brightly coloured ball. Skye went down the terrace steps and walked towards the pool, but as she did so the ball came flying towards her and landed at her feet. A man immediately surged out after it, pushing himself out of the pool in one swift, strong movement. He shook his head to clear the water from his eyes, a spray of drops flying from his hair like liquid crystals in the sun, and she saw that it was Thane. He saw her at the same moment and became suddenly still, standing there with the water running down his body, tall and strong and bronzed by the sun. Their eyes met for a long moment, and then Skye stooped to pick up the ball and hold it out to him, almost as if she was making some offering to a god of the sea. Slowly he reached to take it, but then someone shouted and Skye blinked and saw Scott at the side of the pool. Without warning, she threw the ball to Scott, who gave a yell of triumph and bore it away. Thane's face hardened as he stared at her, his hands falling to his sides. Then he turned without a word and dived back into the pool to chase after Scott.

Aunt Helen was superintending the preparations for a barbecue over in the shade of the trees, and Skye went over to help her. Some more people arrived and Uncle John came over, putting a butcher's apron over his bathing trunks and taking over the cooking. He put steaks and chicken portions, chops and hamburgers on the hot grill, the smoke rising into the still air.

'Hi.' Turning from the salad she was tossing, Skye found Scott beside her. 'You OK now? Jodi said you weren't feeling too good.'

'It was just a headache. I'm fine now, thanks. How about you? How was New York?'

'Hot, humid and smelly. Why our forefathers ever built the biggest city in America in a spot with such a terrible climate, I'll never know.'

He went on to tell her about a court case he'd had to attend where the air-conditioning had broken down and two people had passed out with the heat before the case was through. Skye listened attentively and kept her eyes on him, trying not to notice that Thane and Jodi had come out of the water and were standing together, Jodi with both her arms round Thane's waist, and Thane with a casual arm around Jodi's shoulders.

Skye said hello to Thane a little later on when they were standing in line for the food. She had been talking to Scott all that time and was still with him, because for once Jodi hadn't come over either to join them or draw him away. Thane's eyes flicked over the two of them as he came up and he said, 'Hello, Skye,' in an offhand, almost cool tone.

She returned the greeting in a similar emotionless manner, trying to hide the stab of hurt at his coolness and the way he almost immediately turned away to talk to someone else. It shouldn't have hurt, of course; she ought really to have been glad, because it made it that much easier to behave impersonally herself, but the pain was there like a physical ache in her heart.

Those first few minutes set the tone for the whole weekend. Skye spent most of her time with Scott, who seemed quite willing to stay by her side, and Jodi and Thane were always together. Even when they went out in a foursome that evening, they soon separated and went their own way, Scott taking Skye to watch the floor-show at Le Cabaret Theatre at the Paradise Island Hotel while Jodi insisted on trying her luck at the gaming tables in the casino.

They met up to drive home together in the early hours of the morning, and Scott got into the back of the car, pulling Skye in beside him. After the floor-show they had danced in a dimly lit club where Scott had held her close, both his arms around her, and had several times nuzzled her neck, so it came as no real surprise to Skye when Scott again took her in his arms in the back of the car. He tried to kiss her, but Skye was too aware of Thane's eyes in the driving mirror and pulled away, sliding across the seat and holding Scott off when he went to reach for her again.

She was surprised that Jodi didn't say anything, when so often on the previous weekend she had been possessive towards both men. Perhaps Thane had said something, Skye surmised, had let her know that he objected to her behaviour. Or maybe he just wanted to give Scott a clear field. That thought made her feel wretched for a moment, but there was no time to dwell on it before they pulled up at the house.

'I'm going for a swim,' Jodi announced. 'How about you three?' She ran up to her room and came back wearing a bikini and the rather gaudy, flower-encrusted bathing hat she habitually wore when swimming late at night. The men followed more slowly, but Jodi waited until they were watching before diving cleanly into the pool.

'Aren't you coming in?' Scott asked, turning to Skye.

'No, I'll watch.'

She lay on one of the loungers and looked up at the sky, listening to the others splashing around and laughing in the pool. She had hardly spoken to Thane today; they could have been strangers thrown together by chance. Well, wasn't that what they were, when you came to work it out? But she didn't feel like that. She felt as if she had known him all her life, that there hadn't been a time when he wasn't the most important part of her life. As she looked up at the stars, brilliant in the heavy velvet

of night, Skye could only wonder in amazement
that her heart and emotions could have been so
completely captured in such a short time.

The sounds from the pool had quietened. A man
loomed suddenly over her and Skye's heart skipped
a beat. But it was only Scott. He stooped to sit on
the edge of her lounger and put a hand on each
side of the back rest. Skye read desire in his eyes
and straightened up, laughingly saying, 'Hey, you're
all wet.'

She tried to look past him to see if Thane and
Jodi were still in the pool, but Scott said softly,
'It's OK, they've gone.'

'Gone? Gone where?'

He laughed a little harshly. 'Where do you
think?' And he bent to kiss her.

Skye didn't resist him. Instead, after a few moments, she put her arms round Scott's neck and,
in his embrace, tried to shut out the pictures in her
mind as she thought of Thane with Jodi. Scott's
kiss deepened at her response and he held her close
against his wet chest, his hands starting to caress
her. But after only a couple of minutes Skye drew
back and, shaking Scott off, got quickly to her feet.
'I'm tired. I think I'll go to bed.'

'A great idea.' Scott stood up and reached for
her again.

'Alone!' Skye put her hands against his chest to
push him away as he tried to put his arms round
her.

'You know you don't mean that.'

'Yes, I do. Please let go of me,' she said firmly.

Scott frowned, then stepped back rather petulantly. 'You want to make up your mind. Girls who

blow hot one minute and cold the next are asking for trouble.'

'Oh, for heaven's sake grow up!' Skye exclaimed in sudden impatience. 'Even you should know by now that not every girl you make a pass at is going to jump into bed with you. Why, I hardly know you!'

She had expected him to be annoyed at her outburst, and wasn't prepared for his sudden grin. 'Well, if I didn't know before, I do now. Tell me, is it because you don't like me, or because you have a boyfriend back home in England?'

'Neither,' Skye admitted. 'You're OK, Scott, it's just that—well, you just don't turn me on, that's all.'

'Ouch.' He pretended to wince. 'For someone who looks as soft as a kitten, you have sharp claws.'

'I'm sorry.'

'Don't be.' He moved forward and touched her arm. 'I like a girl who stands up for herself.'

She nodded, hesitated for a moment, then said, 'Goodnight, Scott,' and turned to mount the outside stairs to go to her room.

The moon was out and she had no difficulty in seeing her way, but just as she neared Jodi's room the door on to the balcony opened and Thane came out, closing the door behind him. Skye gave a little gasp and he swung round to face her. For a moment they were both still, then Thane said, 'Are you all right?'

There was a sharpness in his tone, but Skye didn't know if it was because he was concerned for her, or because he was annoyed that she'd seen him leave

Jodi's room. 'Yes,' she answered unsteadily. 'I'm—
I'm fine. Goodnight.'

She walked past and didn't look back until she
reached the corner, then her eyes were drawn ir-
resistibly towards him. He was still standing outside
Jodi's door, watching her. Would he go back in
again when she'd gone? Skye wondered, and felt
an insane stab of jealousy. Biting her lip, she went
quickly on to her room and closed and locked the
windows, pulling the curtains across as if trying to
shut out her thoughts.

Skye didn't expect to enjoy the next day, but
strangely she had a wonderful time. They all four
went down to the beach, where they met up with
some of Jodi's friends who'd been at the barbecue,
and they hired bicycles with huge plastic wheels that
floated on the sea, and then the men had a jet-ski
race. It was a hectic race with no holds barred, and
the girls whooped with laughter as they watched
from the shore. One of the local boys won, but
only because Scott and Thane had spent too much
time trying to push each other off their machines.
At lunchtime they picnicked on the sand, and
afterwards hired tiny sail-boats with brilliantly
striped triangular sails—sunfish, the others called
them. Skye went with Scott, who insisted she wear
a life-jacket, and they sat close together as Scott
steered the little boat over that incredibly blue water.
It was fun, great fun, and Skye felt relaxed and
almost happy. Scott had made no attempt to kiss
her or make a pass today, and when he did touch
her it was only as any person would who was
teaching you a new sport. So Skye was able to enjoy

herself, to lift her face to the breeze and wonder at the beauty of the island as she saw it from the sea.

Perhaps because they understood one another better now, she and Scott were able to talk more freely, and he told her of his life in New York and some of his hopes for the future. Basically these didn't differ much from Thane's, but Skye could sense that they were far more important to Scott. He *had* to get where he wanted to go, and his whole life was geared up to that end. OK, he took time out to come down to the Bahamas to relax, but, if an opportunity came to further his ambitions which would stop him coming here, she couldn't see him hesitating over the choice for a second. And she had an idea that his temperament could soon sour if he felt that he wasn't getting what he wanted, or wasn't getting there fast enough.

'Are you and Thane on the same level in your law firm?' she asked curiously. 'You're not rivals?'

'No, more often than not we help each other out. But then we're still comparative juniors. Maybe as we go higher we'll be battling for the best cases.'

Which meant that they certainly would be, Skye guessed, and wondered if their friendship could stand the test. A thought which made her say, 'You used to go out with Jodi, didn't you?'

'Who told you that?'

'She did.'

Scott gave a twisted grin and pulled on the steering rope to make them avoid a windsurfer. 'Yes, we used to date. But then she fell for Thane.' He shrugged. 'I haven't had a steady date since then.' He looked pensive for a moment, then abruptly changed the subject. 'You want to try and steer?'

Gingerly they changed places and had another pleasant hour before they turned the boat in and joined the others on the beach. Somebody produced cans of beer and the afternoon developed into a beach party, but presently Thane came over to where Skye was sitting and squatted down beside her.

'Scott and I have to leave to catch the plane to New York. If you want to stay on at the party, I'm sure one of the guys will give you a ride back to the house later on.'

'No. Thanks, but I'd rather go back with you now.'

'OK.' Thane stood up, then stretched down his arm to help her to her feet.

It was the first time he had touched her the whole weekend. Skye's hand trembled as she put it in his, and it was all she could to murmur a casual, 'Thanks,' and walk across the sand with him to where Jodi and Scott were waiting, making sure that she walked apart from him so that they didn't touch again.

It was almost a relief when they left this time. Skye didn't go to the airport to see them off, but she stood on the balcony looking up at the sky, knowing that the plane she presently saw climbing away from the island was carrying Thane back to New York. And next week at this time she would be going with him. That was a heart-stopping thought. For a whole week she would be within a short cab ride of him. And he of Jodi. Had the two of them spent last night together? The jealous thought came back to prick at her brain. Well, what if they had? Skye told herself sternly. They were engaged to be married, weren't they? If they wanted to go to bed together, it was none of her damn business. But somehow even that firm self-chastisement didn't help a bit, and Skye went to bed wishing that she'd never come to Nassau.

The sun and the idle life-style had made Skye feel much better physically, and during the next week she ventured to do some gentle swimming in the pool. Jodi and her mother were terribly busy with wedding preparations. They went to the cathedral to arrange the wedding service and for a rehearsal a few days before, photographs of wedding bouquets and church decorations were studied and chosen, seating plans for the reception were drawn up provisionally, only to be changed the next day as an invitation was refused or they remembered that two people they'd put next to each other were no longer on speaking terms. More presents arrived at the house and were put out on display in Uncle John's study, with little cards in front of each one to say who had sent them.

Skye watched it all and wondered what her own wedding might be like. In a church, of course, but nothing as grand as a cathedral. And presumably she would wear a white dress and there would be a reception. Skye could visualise all that, but when it came to imagining the man standing beside her in all this there was only one face she could picture. So maybe any wedding at all was out of the question. That was a difficult thought to push aside when she was in the midst of the wedding preparations for Thane and Jodi, but she did her best, and got a great deal of work done that week. She collected her painting from the framer's and gave it to her uncle when he came with Thane and Scott the following weekend.

He was enthusiastic about it. 'A delightful painting,' he declared. 'You have real talent. How strange that the creative instinct in you should have come out for art rather than for music, like your parents. This will hang in pride of place in my office.'

Uncle John was so pleased with the picture that he showed it to a group of friends who came round for drinks that evening. They, too, thought it was good, and two of them even asked Skye to paint similar pictures for them. And it wasn't that they were merely being polite or wanted to please Uncle John; they offered her definite commissions and a good price. Skye was pleased and flattered, but had to refuse. 'I'm only on holiday here,' she explained, 'and there probably won't be time before I go home.'

'But you could stay on after the wedding,' Aunt Helen interrupted. 'And I'd love it if you did. I shall be so lonely here without Jodi. Especially after all the excitement of the wedding.'

Her uncle added his voice to his wife's invitation, but Skye would only thank them without committing herself, although she did promise to try to do at least one of the paintings if she had time after she got back from New York.

Thane had been standing on the edge of the group, listening, and when the others moved away came to stand beside her. To Skye's hungry eyes he seemed to look even more handsome tonight. He was wearing a dark suit and casual jacket that made his face look thinner than she'd remembered, the strong lines of his cheeks and jaw more distinctive, the cleft in his chin more deeply shadowed. 'Knowing the number of wealthy people who live or have holiday homes on the island,' he remarked, 'I reckon you could make a living here just by painting pictures like that.'

'I think I might get tired of it after a while,' Skye answered lightly. 'I like to have some variety in my work.'

'But you could do enough to extend your vacation, couldn't you?'

'I have commitments in England I have to get home for. I've already been away quite a long time.'

'Commitments?' Thane leaned against the wall, his eyes on her face. 'Do you mean a man—a boyfriend?'

'No.' Skye shook her head with a ghost of a smile. 'I mean work that I'm under contract to do.'

'Couldn't you do it here? Jodi tells me that you've been working while you've been staying with her parents.'

Skye glanced quickly up at him, wondering why he was saying this, almost as if he was encouraging her to stay. There was an intent look in his eyes, but it was one she couldn't fathom. She shook her head dismissively. 'It wouldn't be the same.' Aware that she had sounded harsh, she added lightly, 'And, anyway, I have a home and family to go back to.'

'Yes, I guess one tends to forget that. Probably because I can only picture you here. Do you love England very much?'

It was a strange question, and one that made Skye turn and look at him fully. They were standing on the terrace and were momentarily alone, most of the other guests having moved inside to eat from the buffet that had just been served. 'Yes, of course. Doesn't everyone love their home?'

Thane gave a rather world-weary smile. 'Not everyone loves their country, no. Some can't wait to leave it, and come to the States, for example.'

'I love mine,' Skye said firmly. 'And I love my family and my life there.'

'So I guess nothing would make you leave it?'

It was almost a statement rather than a question, and Skye needn't have answered, but there was something in his voice, perhaps again an inflection of heaviness, that made her say, 'Only one thing, I suppose.' Thane looked at her enquiringly, his head lifted in sudden interest, and she added, 'If something or—someone came to mean more to me, then I would be willing to leave. I would miss it terribly, of course, but I think that you have to follow your heart. Don't you?' And she lifted dark, vulnerable eyes to look at him.

He didn't speak at once, and when he did Thane didn't give her a straight answer, instead saying, 'I think you must be the most unselfish person I've ever met.'

Skye gave a startled, laughing gasp. 'Oh, but I...' Her voice died, her pulses beginning to race as she looked into his intent face. She remembered that he'd once said that she and Jodi were completely different, and wondered if he was comparing them. Shaking her head, she said, 'I'm sure I'm just as

selfish as anyone else. You just don't know me very
well.'

He looked as if he was going to say something,
but changed his mind and straightened up rather
abruptly. 'No, I guess not. Let's go in and eat, shall
we?'

It had been a strange few minutes of conversation. Skye pondered it for the rest of the evening,
but she didn't speak to Thane again. In fact, he
almost seemed to be avoiding her, much as he had
done last weekend. Skye was unable to keep her
eyes away from him for very long, so that sometimes their glances met, but whenever they did they
both looked quickly away. Skye sensed a brooding
restlessness in Thane. It wasn't something she could
put her finger on: he behaved completely naturally
as he talked to the guests, but some instinct made
her feel that this was only a façade and that something was on his mind. Skye turned her attention
to Jodi, trying to see if she, too, was feeling
troubled, but her cousin was in the best of spirits,
laughing with the guests, thanking those who'd
given her wedding presents, and talking excitedly
about the wedding and the coming trip to New
York. Whatever was fretting Thane certainly wasn't
troubling Jodi, so presumably she didn't know
about it. If there was anything at all, of course; it
might be that Skye herself was being over-sensitive.

The guests stayed late that evening, and Skye felt
tired when she went to bed. It was a very hot, humid
night, and she left the air-conditioning on, but its
vibrant whirr, although low, kept her awake and
eventually made her head start to ache. Getting up,
she opened the curtains and pushed the windows

open, letting in what little breeze there was. A full
moon glowed in the sky, its features smiling on this
favoured land, and Skye stepped out on to the
balcony to get a better view. From the pool came
faint splashing sounds. Scott and Thane, she pre-
sumed, having a cool swim before turning in; Jodi
had come up at the same time as herself. A slight
noise in the garden made her turn and look down.
She had been wrong; Thane wasn't in the pool. He
was walking in the garden, still fully dressed, his
hands in his pockets and making no attempt now
to hide the fact that something was troubling him.
He walked with his head bent, his eyes on the
ground, pacing slowly across the lawn; whatever
the problem was, it lay heavily on his shoulders.
He reached the end of the lawn, stood broodingly
for a minute, and then turned, looking up as he
did so. But Skye had slipped back into her room
and closed the windows quietly behind her. There
was nothing she could do, she had no right to offer
comfort or even a willing ear to listen; that was
Jodi's privilege, not hers. But, even so, she longed
with all her heart to share his trouble, to ease it if
she could.

The following day was another scorcher and
made everyone feel rather listless. Uncle John cancelled a round of golf that he'd arranged with three
friends, and took them and their wives, with Aunt
Helen, out on the boat instead. Jodi and Thane
had an appointment with one of the cathedral of-
ficials to discuss the arrangements for the wedding
service and to have what Jodi termed 'a pre-nuptial
pep talk'. Then they were going to have lunch with
a friend of Jodi's. So that left Scott and Skye alone

for the day. They were invited to join the boat trip, but decided they were the wrong generation and went down to Paradise Beach instead. Mostly they sat in the shade of the Casuarina trees that lined the beach because the sun was just too hot, but later in the afternoon Scott hired another sunfish and they went sailing again.

'Mm,' Skye remarked as they picked up a sea breeze and skidded across the water, 'I could really get to like this. It's the first time I've felt cool all day.'

Scott grinned and ducked under the isosceles triangle sail of red, orange and yellow stripes. They were both wearing life-jackets, but Scott had stopped in the straw market to buy large-brimmed hats to protect their necks and faces, and insisted on their putting large dollops of screening cream on their noses. Skye was sure they made a comical-looking pair, but she didn't care, it was too hot to care.

They talked lazily, at ease with each other because there wasn't any sexual tension, and Skye said, 'Are you working on a big case now?'

'Nothing special. There are always a lot of company cases going on, but I don't think anything's around that's different from normal.'

'How about Thane? Is he working on anything big?'

'No, I'm certain he isn't. The firm wouldn't give him anything like that right now, not when he's soon going to take a couple of months off for his honeymoon vacation.' Scott frowned against the sun as he looked at her. 'Why do you ask?'

'Oh, no reason, really. I just thought Thane seemed rather preoccupied yesterday.'

'Yeah? Can't say that I noticed. He seemed the same as usual to me. But then he isn't the kind of guy who tells you every little thing. Maybe I'll ask him when he gets back.'

'Oh, no, please don't do that.' Skye protested too quickly. 'I expect I'm just imagining it.'

'Maybe so.' But Scott gave her an intent look before turning to steer the boat back to the shore.

They were the last home. Uncle John was in good spirits because he'd caught a large blackfin which he'd brought home for them to see before he handed it over to the cook to prepare for the next day. They had had a marvellous day, Aunt Helen told them, and were going to a dance at the golf club with their friends after dinner. Jodi was up in her room when Skye got home, so on her way up to her own room she knocked on her cousin's door and poked her head in. 'Hi. You decent?'

'What? Oh, yes, come in.'

Jodi was sitting at her dressing-table, cleaning off her face, her mouth in a moody, downward curve.

'How did your day go?' Skye asked, sitting on the bed.

'All right, I suppose. I'll be glad when the whole thing's over,' Jodi added pettishly.

Skye gave her a wary look; usually Jodi was only too pleased to discuss any aspect of the wedding, and loved every minute of the preparations. 'Can't you have the service you wanted?'

'Oh, yes. It's going to be exactly as I worked it out beforehand. And I had my choice of the hymns and music.'

'Thane agreed with what you'd chosen, evidently?'

Jodi suddenly flung down the cleansing pad she was using, and swung round to face her. 'You can hardly say agreed!' she exclaimed angrily. 'He hardly said a word the whole time we were there. I don't know why he bothered to go with me at all. Whenever I asked for his opinion he just said, "Do what you want." I just don't know what's got into him lately.'

'Perhaps he was feeling the heat,' Skye suggested lamely, but Jodi brushed that remark away with the contempt it deserved.

'Of course he wasn't. He was OK until we saw the priest who gave us a lecture on what marriage stood for and how we should always communicate with one another and forgive each other's faults and all that kind of nonsense.'

'Hardly nonsense,' Skye broke in.

'Oh, you know what I mean; it was entirely unnecessary. Everyone knows what marriage is for, for heaven's sake. The church seems to still think we're back in the Dark Ages.'

'But you want to be married in a church,' Skye pointed out gently.

'Well, of course. Anyone who's anyone gets married in the cathedral in Nassau because it holds so many more people. Hardly anyone would see your dress if you got married in one of the little churches or at home.'

Skye was silent, taken aback by Jodi's reasoning, and her cousin went on, 'Anyway, as I was saying, Thane was OK until we had the pep talk, then he just clammed up and wouldn't show any interest in the ceremony when we went to discuss that later.'

She grumbled some more but Skye was no longer listening; her thoughts were full of Thane, her mind troubled. 'Didn't you ask him what was the matter?' she ventured.

'I tried to, but he wouldn't tell me. Oh, I hate it when men go moody on you,' she added petulantly.

Refraining from asking any more questions, Skye wisely left her cousin alone and went to change for dinner.

It wasn't an easy meal; there was a brittle kind of tension between Jodi and Thane that communicated to all of them. Jodi was openly sulking and refused to look at Thane, instead giving her attention to Scott.

It was the housekeeper's night off, so to avoid the atmosphere in the dining-room Skye went into the kitchen with her aunt to help make the coffee.

'Oh, dear,' Aunt Helen sighed, 'I hope those two haven't had a fight. Still, I expect it's only pre-wedding nerves, don't you?'

'I wouldn't know. Have they—have they had rows before?'

'Not really. But all couples have spats from time to time.'

Skye supposed she was right, although her own parents were very happy and contented, with each other and with their lives, and she had never known them to have a real fight. Disagreements, sometimes, over minor things, but never one of those serious quarrels where people hurled abuse and acted as if they hated each other.

She carried the coffee-tray into the sitting-room, and her aunt and uncle drank theirs quickly and went up to change for the dance at the golf club. When they'd gone, Jodi said, 'Where shall we go tonight? How about the Cable Beach casino? Or we could go to a nightclub. What do you think, Scott?'

He shrugged. 'I'm easy. How about you, Skye?'

'Isn't it a little hot for dancing? Why don't we go down to the beach and take a walk along the sand or build a fire out of driftwood?'

'Oh, that's kids' stuff,' Jodi cut in impatiently. 'Nobody does that kind of thing any more.'

'Well, maybe they should,' Thane said shortly. 'Maybe it's about time we all got back to basics.'

'If getting back to basics means slumming around on a beach when we could be at a nightclub, then you can keep it,' Jodi fired back. The colour had heightened in her cheeks and she was really angry. 'For heaven's sake, Thane, what's the point of you coming here unless it's so we can go out and have a good time?' Thane was silent, his mouth drawn into a thin line, and Jodi suddenly realised what she'd said. Running to him, she threw her arms round Thane's neck. 'Oh, I'm sorry, darling. But I just don't understand you tonight. We always go to a club or something when you're here; why should tonight be any different?'

She was right in a way, Skye thought; as far as Jodi was concerned, this weekend *was* the same as any other, but she just couldn't see that it was Thane himself who wanted it to be different.

In the end Jodi had her way and they went to the casino at Cable Beach. This wasn't as grand as the one on Paradise Island, there were more ordinary tourists dressed in casual holiday clothes and the stakes weren't so high. They all gambled a little. Jodi wanted to play roulette, but Skye moved from table to table, trying out all the different games. Scott came with her part of the time, but he, too, liked roulette and went back to join the others. After about half an hour or so, though, he came up to Skye where she was seated at the blackjack table and put a hand on her arm, saying, 'Skye, we have to go.'

Surprised by the seriousness of his tone, Skye immediately got to her feet. 'Why? What's happened?'

'You'll see.' Taking her arm, he led her over to a roulette table on the far side of the room. Thane and Jodi were standing just behind the seated players, and it was obvious that they'd had a row. Jodi's face was red and belligerent, Thane's pale and grim.

As Skye came up, she heard Jodi say in a fierce undertone, 'I will *not* go home! I'll stay here as long as I damn well like!'

Her voice was slightly slurred, and Skye could tell by the looseness in her face that she'd been drinking. As soon as Skye and Scott joined them, Thane took hold of Jodi's arm and tried to lead her to the exit, but she hung back and glared at him defiantly. 'I am not leaving. If I want to gamble, that's my affair. It isn't your money, it's mine. And I can...'

Her words were broken off as Thane suddenly gave an exclamation of impatience, picked Jodi up and slung her over his shoulder, then marched to the door, completely ignoring the grinning onlookers.

When they reached the car, Thane just dumped Jodi in the front seat and got in beside her while Scott and Skye went in the back. Jodi was absolutely furious, with embarrassment as much as anything. She rounded on Thane and accused him of making her a laughing-stock in front of the whole island. He just told her to shut up in a voice that was so cold it made even Skye shiver, and Jodi relapsed into a sulky silence. At the house, Skye took Jodi upstairs and put her to bed, shutting her ears to her cousin's complaints and sobs of self-pity, then went along to her own room. It had been quite a night.

Skye took off most of her clothes, and lay on top of her bed, feeling hot and trying to push all thoughts of Thane and Jodi's row from her mind. It was too hot to get into the bed, too hot to sleep. After half an hour or so she couldn't stand it any longer, and changed into her swim-suit and went down to the pool. There was no one else there. Skye began to pin up her cloud of dark hair, but then saw Jodi's cap lying on a lounger and decided to borrow that instead.

The water felt fantastic, delicious, the heat slipping from her body and leaving her feeling cool at last. She swam gently, mindful of her appendix scar, only doing one length at a time then stopping to rest. The night was quiet, the only sounds the night birds and the distant hum of traffic carried on the night breeze. Skye reached the end of the pool and, holding on to the side, dipped her head into the water to cool off, her eyes closed, amusing herself by seeing how many she could count to before she had to come up for air.

So she didn't hear someone dive into the water, didn't know anyone was there until a pair of arms grabbed hold of her and lifted her head out of the water, a hand under her chin. She gave a cry of alarm which was broken off as she saw that it was Thane. Then suddenly she was in his arms and his mouth was on hers. With a moan of amazed gladness, Skye instinctively returned his kiss, responding with the fierce longing of an impossible dream that had suddenly come true.

CHAPTER FIVE

THAT kiss was so intense, so passionate, that Skye felt even hotter than she had out of the water. There had been a brief moment when Thane had stood transfixed, but then his arms tightened around her and he held her close against him as he kissed her with equal urgency. Skye's eyes were closed and she felt as if she were drowning, drowning in his closeness, drowning in the touch of his lips as they pressed against her own, hard and possessive, demanding and receiving a total surrender. Time and common sense were lost as all the deep, aching need that had been building up inside her over the past weeks was suddenly released in a flame of passionate hunger.

When at last he released her Skye kept her eyes closed, her senses floating on the water around her, not wanting it to end. Not wanting to face reality, because for her, now, the only reality she would ever find would be in Thane's arms. But then he said her name on a husky note, and she reluctantly opened her eyes.

'I'm sorry,' Thane said hollowly. 'I was sure you were Jodi. I saw her hat, and you had your head in the water—I thought Jodi had gone for a swim and had got into trouble. She was pretty drunk, and I thought...' His unsteady voice came to a stop as he stared at her. 'I guess—I guess you thought

I was Scott?' Again his voice was unsteady, questioning.

Skye looked at him for a long moment, opened her mouth to speak, then abruptly turned and swam to the nearby steps where she hauled herself out of the water.

'Skye?' Thane came quickly up behind her and put a hand on her arm, stopping her when she would have run in.

She turned, putting up a hand to pull off the bathing cap, and then realised that Thane was wearing nothing but a pair of pyjama trousers that clung wetly to his body, emphasising his manhood and the muscular strength of his legs. A sick feeling of anguish hit her as she realised the mistake he'd made. He had thought she was Jodi all along. His hand was still on her arm as he was waiting for her answer, for reassurance. And it would have been so easy to accept the excuse he'd offered her, to lie and by so doing salvage something of her own pride and dignity. But to save it by a lie... Lifting her head, Skye said in a tight, wretched voice, 'No, I— I knew it was you. I'm sorry. I'm—so, so sorry.' And then she pulled her arm free and turned to run up the steps to the balcony and the sanctuary of her own room, while Thane stood staring after her.

She didn't sleep much that night, but Skye rose early and walked down into Nassau to go to the early church service. Mostly she prayed for the strength to resist and hide this love she felt for Thane, and she prayed, too, for the will-power to accept that he would never be hers and to wish him and Jodi genuine happiness when she stood behind them and watched them exchange their vows on their wedding day. It wouldn't be long, she comforted herself, just a few weeks now, and that major ordeal to get through, and then she would be able to go home and put all this behind her. Not to forget, but at least to try and build some kind of future for herself, although when you knew you could never share it with the man you loved there seemed little point to it. No, she mustn't think that way. She must be very, very positive. Because if she wasn't . . . Skye had a brief glimpse over the edge of pain and despair, and pulled herself sharply back, feeling suddenly and terribly afraid.

As she walked home along the sunlit, tree-lined roads, Skye blamed herself for being such a weak fool last night. She had known it was Thane, and she should have made herself known—pushed him away or something when he grabbed her. But she hadn't, and now everything would be different between them. Coming to a sudden standstill, Skye realised that she not only had to see and be near him today, but also during the coming week in New York. Her courage failed her at the thought. She couldn't do it. She just couldn't. Even before it would have been exquisite torture, but now—it was just impossible. But she couldn't turn tail and run home, not when she'd promised to be a bridesmaid. It would be letting Jodi down, as well as her aunt and uncle. And what excuse could she possibly give? I'm sorry, I'm too much in love with the bridegroom to take part in his wedding?

Slowly she began to walk on again, dragging out the moment before she reached the house. But she had to reach it eventually and found everyone in the garden, having a late breakfast.

'Skye, dear, do come and sit down. I got your note. Did you enjoy the church service? They're quite spirited here on the island, aren't they?'

Skye glanced at her aunt to see if the pun had been intentional, but saw it hadn't and sat down beside her. 'Very,' she agreed gravely, and looked up to see Thane's lips quirking with laughter. He caught her eye and grinned, but suddenly remembered the night before and the laughter faded. Immediately Skye turned to greet the others, her heart contracting. Jodi's eyes were dark-shadowed, and it was soon obvious that she knew she'd made a fool of herself last night; she was sitting next to Thane and was making a great fuss of him, pouring out his coffee and behaving like a bride on the first morning after the wedding. Whether Thane was pleased about this, Skye didn't know, because she didn't look directly at him again, but there was no tension in the air so she gathered that everything was fine between them again.

Everyone just lazed around in the sun that morning. Skye sat in the shade and worked on her sketch-pad, filling in detail on the drawings she'd done, while the others played tennis. At lunchtime they all drove over to a barbecue party at the house of some friends of Aunt Helen at Lyford Cay. It was on a private estate and was very luxurious, even by her aunt and uncle's standards. Skye watched Jodi looking round and could almost see her cousin's mind working as she determined to have a place like this herself one day.

Among so many people it was easy to lose herself, and easy to take an occasional glance at Thane in the hope that it wouldn't be noticed. He looked particularly devastating today, dressed in well-cut casual trousers and an open-necked shirt with the cuffs turned back. He looked what he was: strong, self-confident, at ease in these rich surroundings and among so many wealthy people. He turned his head suddenly and met her eyes, and for a brief moment his face seemed as vulnerable as her own.

But it could only have been an illusion, of course; Jodi spoke to him and pulled at his sleeve, and he turned away to resume his conversation.

Shaken, Skye walked over to her uncle, but he was talking business with a group of men, and her aunt was talking weddings with several other middle-aged women.

'I know exactly what you're thinking. Bet you ten dollars I'm right.' Scott came up to stand beside Skye and grinned down at her.

'OK, you're on. What am I thinking?'

'That if you hear another word about the wedding you'll scream. And,' he held up a finger when she went to speak, 'what wouldn't you give to be out of this heat and back home in cold, wet England. Well, do I get my ten dollars?'

Skye laughed and said, 'You most certainly do. I can see I shall have to be careful what I'm thinking in future.' And she took her purse from her bag and held out a ten-dollar bill. 'They'll have to be Bahamian dollars, I'm afraid.'

Scott gave her a surprised look. 'It was only a joke, you don't have to pay me.'

'Nonsense, a bet is a bet.' And she slipped the money into a pocket in his shirt when he refused to take it.

'What was the bet?' Jodi came up to them, still hanging on to Thane's arm.

'Skye will tell you,' Scott said smoothly, and grinned mendaciously.

'Coward!' Skye gave him an indignant glance. 'He bet he knew what I was thinking and he was right, that's all.'

'So what were you thinking?' Jodi demanded bluntly.

Ducking out of the whole truth, Skye said, 'That the heat was getting a bit too much for me.'

'Now who's a coward?' Scott whispered in her ear.

Skye gave a light laugh and found Thane watching her, his jaw set almost grimly. But Jodi was saying, 'You think this is hot? You wait till we get to New York.'

'Talking of New York,' Scott cut in smoothly, 'isn't it time we were leaving?'

Her luggage for the trip was already packed, but when they got back to the house Skye hastily added some more casual clothes and her sketching things to the case. Because she was going to take the coward's way out. The idea had come to her earlier, but had solidified during the course of the day: she would go to New York with the others and be fitted with the bridesmaid's dress, but as soon as that was done she would take off on her own and not come back to Nassau until the eve of the wedding. She would make the excuse that she wanted to go on a painting and sketching trip, and as she was over twenty-one there really wasn't anything her aunt and uncle could do to stop her. If it came to it, she might even be super-cowardly and just leave a note.

So long as she made it for the wedding ceremony, what did it matter?

It did matter, of course; Skye knew that, but she just couldn't face a whole week of seeing Thane, and then a couple more weekends with him in the same house in the Bahamas, before he came down with his family a few days before the wedding. Skye just knew she couldn't do it; she had always been brought up to be open and honest, and she just didn't think she could hide her feelings, because doing so was almost a form of deception and she had no experience of that.

Feeling happier in her mind, she drove with the others to the airport and sat next to Scott on the plane. In New York they split up and she went with the Bentons to their Manhattan apartment. It was very modern, the kitchen full of electrical gadgets Skye had never seen before, and she had fun trying them all out. Most of the time only Uncle John used the apartment regularly, so it wasn't very large and Skye and Jodi had to share a room. They unpacked together, Jodi finding a few inches of space in her wardrobes for the few things Skye had brought with her.

'I'll have to leave most of these things here until we can find a bigger apartment,' Jodi muttered.

'Aren't you going to live in Thane's apartment?'

'No, it really isn't big enough. I'm hoping we'll have time to look round for a new place this week. Although there's no real hurry until we get back from our honeymoon. Perhaps Mummy will have time to look round for us while we're away.'

'Don't you and Thane want to find your own place?' Skye asked in surprise.

'Oh, but Mummy has far more time than us. And she has excellent taste.'

Skye had to agree with that, but privately thought that a major part of the fun of getting married would be looking together for somewhere to live. But such thoughts were both unwise and disloyal. Skye pushed them out of her head as much as she could and prepared to enjoy New York.

They had been right about the heat: every pavement and wall seemed to act like a radiator and bounce back at you. Aunt Helen took her sightseeing the first morning, but after only a few hours Skye had had enough and was thankful to retreat to the air-conditioned coolness of a fashionable restaurant for lunch. Her aunt picked at her food as usual, ever-mindful of her figure, and spent most of the time looking round for celebrities or people she knew. But even she had found the heat enervating and didn't take much persuasion to drop Skye off at an art gallery while she went by cab to do some shopping.

Wandering around the rooms in the gallery, studying the paintings and pieces of sculpture, helped Skye to get back her sense of perspective. Nassau had been so exotic, so romantic, a place made for love to blossom, but New York brought you swiftly back to reality, and she saw that there was no place for her here. Jodi and Thane were right for each other and she was the odd one out. Because her world was one of creativity and the pleasure of looking at beautiful paintings like these, whereas theirs was one of commercialism and law, of gaining money and power, and trying to win for your side when men or companies went into legal battles. But, although she saw all that, it didn't stop her loving Thane, nothing could, and Skye knew that in opting to leave New York as soon as possible she had made the right decision.

There was to be a big family get-together that evening. Thane's parents and sister were coming to town, and they were all going to have dinner at a restaurant. Jodi was excited about it, but her mother was anxious in case Thane's parents didn't agree with the wedding arrangements she'd made. 'They're so intellectual,' she fretted. 'I never know what they're talking about half the time. And even if they say they're pleased about something, I never feel as if they really are. Still, as we're paying for the wedding, there really isn't very much they can object to, is there?'

'Oh, Mummy, don't worry about it,' Jodi told her. 'I'm sure they'll be pleased with all you've arranged. I just hope Angie will wear the colours I've chosen for the bridesmaids' dresses.'

It was in this tense kind of mood that they went to the restaurant to meet the Tyson family, plus Scott of course, only to find that they were early and the others hadn't yet arrived. 'I told you we needn't have hurried,' Uncle John grumbled. 'It's only a quarter to eight.'

But luckily the Tysons were early too. Skye saw Thane walk into the bar in his white dinner-jacket and fell in love with him all over again. Her heart jolted so much that for a few breathless seconds she couldn't tear her eyes from him, but then she remembered and hastily looked away. Scott came after Thane and gave her a strange look, but then her attention was drawn to Thane's parents. Mr and

Mrs Tyson were about ten years older than Aunt
Helen and Uncle John, and much less fashionable.
They looked as if they were quite happy to have
settled into middle age and grey hair, and their
manner was easy and relaxed. The two sets of
parents greeted each other warmly, although Jodi's
were far more effusive. And then Thane's sister,
Angie, a tall, slim blonde, stepped forward to shake
hands. And after that it was Skye's turn to be
introduced.

She shook hands and said hello in her calm, soft
voice, and received looks of genuine interest when
her aunt introduced her as the artist in the family.
Skye managed to laugh that off and turned to say
hello to Scott. He kissed her on the cheek instead
of taking the hand she held out to him and, after
the briefest hesitation, Thane did too. Skye felt his
eyes on her when he stepped back, but somehow
she willed herself not to look at him, instead turning
away to ask Angie if she lived in New York.

'Well, no, at the moment I'm commuting from
Maryland every day, but now that the job I've got
seems to be working out, I plan to take over Thane's
apartment when he moves out.'

'And take over my rent, of course,' Thane put
in.

The tension eased as they all laughed, and the
conversation became general until they went in to
dinner. They had been given a large round table,
and Aunt Helen, as the hostess, told everyone where
to sit, putting herself next to Mr Tyson and Uncle
John between Angie and Mrs Tyson. Skye found
herself between Angie and Thane. In Nassau she
had always sat next to Scott, and had taken care

to avoid being next to Thane, but it wouldn't really
have mattered if there hadn't been those few, passionate moments in the pool that neither of them
could forget. Now that memory created an
awareness between them that couldn't be dispelled.
If Skye hadn't run away immediately after her pa-
thetic admission that she'd known it was Thane, if
they had had an opportunity to discuss it, perhaps
it wouldn't have been so bad. But it hadn't been
just a friendly kiss, or even a passing opportunity
taken; they both knew that it had meant far more
than that, to Skye at least, and it was very difficult
to try to pretend that it had never happened.

Skye spent most of the meal talking to Angie,
whom she liked instantly, but it was inevitable that
Thane should turn to Skye when he wasn't talking
to Jodi. He spoke to her and watched her face while
he listened to her reply. He smiled and laughed,
and grew suddenly pensive. It was inevitable, too,
that their hands or knees sometimes touched, and
Thane's eyes flew to her face when she quickly
pulled away. A waiter dropped a plate and the
maître d' told him off in a display of silent his-
trionics that was so funny, Skye couldn't resist bor-
rowing Thane's pen and doing a lightning sketch
of the two on the back of a menu. Thane leaned
closer to look, his shoulder touching hers, his face
only a few inches away, and suddenly Skye's hand
began to tremble so that it took an enormous effort
of will to finish the drawing.

'Say, that's really clever,' Angie commented.

Skye was grateful to turn to her, aware that she
had almost betrayed her feelings yet again. She
found that Angie was almost as knowledgeable

about art as she was herself, and of course knew a great deal about American painters.

'I saw the work of some in a gallery this afternoon and it made me realise how ignorant I am,' Skye admitted.

'Then you must let me lend you some books,' Angie offered eagerly. 'I have a whole shelf full of books on American art back home.'

'That's very kind of you, and ordinarily I'd love to borrow some, but—well, I'm not going to be in New York for very long.' Skye lowered her voice a little, not yet having told anyone of her plans to take off as soon as she could.

'That's OK, you can let me have them back when I come down to Nassau for the wedding. I'll bring some into work with me tomorrow and give them to Thane to bring over tomorrow night when he visits Jodi. You can pick them up from my office, can't you, Thane?' she added, looking at her brother.

'Sure.' His eyes settled on Skye. 'Why don't you two take in some more art galleries while Skye is here? Then she could really get to know our *colonial* and *primitive* art.'

Skye laughed, enjoying his teasing. 'Can I help it if you have so few well-known artists compared to Europe? There are so many of those to study that there was hardly time for any others.'

'What are you talking about? Oh, not art again!' Jodi was leaning over to listen, her shoulder familiarly against Thane's, her voice becoming bored.

'So what's wrong in art?' There was a distinct challenge in Thane's voice as he turned to Jodi.

Quickly she dissembled. 'Why, nothing, of course. Daddy's really pleased with his picture that Skye painted for him.' And she began to tell Mr Tyson, on her other side, all about it.

There was a small dance-floor in the restaurant. A few couples got up to gyrate slowly round to the music, but surprisingly the first people from their table to take to the floor were Mr and Mrs Tyson.

'They just love dancing,' Angie remarked with affection strong in her voice. 'There's just no holding them back when there's a dance band around.'

Following their elders' example, Scott danced with Skye and then with Angie, while Thane of course danced with Jodi. But he only danced with her once and then sat drinking his coffee, seeming to concentrate on his parents as they happily circled the floor.

'They're good,' Skye commented.

Thane turned to her and smiled. 'Mm. They were brought up on all that quickstep and foxtrot stuff.'

'I read somewhere that ballroom dancing was having a revival. Maybe we'd better all start learning it,' Skye remarked. 'We don't want our parents leaving us behind.'

'Definitely not.' Thane raised an eyebrow. 'Want to try it?'

'Oh, but I didn't mean...'

'No—but I did.' And he held his hand out towards her, palm uppermost.

Before Skye could answer, Jodi caught hold of his other arm and said, 'Come on, let's dance.'

Skye was sure that Jodi was unaware that Thane had already asked *her*, but there was a tiny frown between his eyes as he said, 'I've just asked Skye.'

'Oh, no, please,' Skye protested quickly. 'If Jodi wants to dance, you must go ahead.'

'But I'm asking *you*.' There was a strange note in Thane's voice, almost of challenge, and his blue eyes held hers steadily.

For all her look of frailty, Skye didn't lack courage, and she would have given anything to have said yes. But her courage failed her now. She was afraid of that note in his voice and afraid of giving herself away completely yet again if she was held in his arms, necessarily close on the small and now rather crowded dance-floor. Her eyes fell before his and she said, 'Thanks, but—but I'm rather tired. It's been a long day.'

She was aware that his eyes stayed on her for a long moment, but then Jodi pulled at his arm again. 'We might as well dance if Skye doesn't feel like it.'

Thane hesitated, then said in a short, almost curt voice, 'Why not?'

When Scott asked her to dance again, Skye had no choice but to refuse, but he seemed quite happy to dance with Angie, renewing their old friendship and talking a lot as they went round the floor. Skye had just one more dance before they left, and that was a slow amble with Uncle John. For a few moments Skye was tempted to tell him then of her decision to leave them in a couple of days, but realised that she was still bound by the way the bridesmaid's dress would fit tomorrow. If it didn't need too much alteration, and therefore another fitting, then she would be free to go. And there seemed little point in telling him and facing his inevitable protests until the need arose.

It was about eleven-thirty when they left the restaurant, the heat hitting them as soon as they came out of the swing doors. One of the buildings on the skyline flashed the temperature, ninety-six degrees, and Skye took her first look at the famous skyscrapers outlined against the darkness of the night, a sight she had so often seen on films or in photographs. But they didn't do it justice, she thought. It was almost like fantasy land when you saw all the brilliantly lit stores and advertising signs and thousands of lit windows in the buildings all around. In some ways it was very like London, of course—it had the same feel of a big city—but it smelt different, sharper somehow, perhaps because the sea was so near.

She became aware of Thane's eyes on her. 'Your first visit to New York?' And, when she nodded, 'Someone ought to take you out on a ferry so that you can see the whole skyline at night. And Liberty, of course. You can't possibly leave New York without seeing that.' There was a note of regret in his voice, and he half turned to Jodi, as if about to suggest they all go.

But Skye said quickly, 'I must make a point of doing that some time. Goodnight. Goodnight, Mr Tyson. Mrs Tyson. I'm so pleased to have met you.'

The goodnights became general then, and Skye went home with her aunt and uncle, and Jodi too, which was rather unexpected—to the others as well, because Aunt Helen said in surprise, 'Isn't Thane going to drive you home?'

'No, he has a busy day tomorrow,' Jodi answered, so shortly that no one dared ask her anything else.

Skye had comforted herself with the knowledge that she might only have tomorrow to get through if the bridesmaid's dress was OK, so it was in some apprehension that she went along with her aunt and cousin the next morning to the fashion house where the dresses were being made. 'I'm going to try my dress on as well,' Jodi said excitedly. 'Just in case I've altered my weight at all since my last fitting. You just can't be too careful.'

Aunt Helen was also having an outfit made, and she tried hers on first, looking extremely smart in a navy and white figured suit and the most gorgeous hat. She smiled in pleasure when both girls spontaneously and sincerely complimented her. 'But what if it rains?' Skye teased.

'It wouldn't dare! Now, off you two go and try your dresses on so that I can see them.'

Skye was shown into a changing cubicle that was almost as big as her bedroom back home in England, and presently an assistant brought the dress in to her. It was a lovely dress, in the palest coral colour with a full skirt, puff sleeves, a quite low, rounded neckline and fastened by lots of tiny little buttons at the back. The assistant had to help her with the buttons, and fastened a head-dress of artificial flowers on to her hair, although the flowers would be real on the day. Then Skye turned and looked at herself in the mirror. She gazed for so long that the assistant murmured a word of apology and went to help someone else.

Her reflection stared back at her, wide-eyed and vulnerable. She looked very lovely, perhaps the best she had ever looked, but Skye wasn't aware of that. She saw herself only as the bridesmaid. And at Thane's wedding. She had known the time would come, of course, and come soon, but nothing had brought home the fact that Thane would be Jodi's husband as much as this moment. She felt an appalling sense of loss; but how could she feel that when Thane had never been hers to lose? But it was there, like a terrible weight in her heart, a burden she knew she would carry for the rest of her life.

'Skye? Aren't you ready? Doesn't it fit?' Her aunt had changed and come looking for her. When she saw Skye gazing in the mirror, she laughed. 'Admiring yourself? You do look very pretty, dear. But come along now, Jodi's waiting.'

Still bemused, Skye turned and followed her out into the private modelling-room. Jodi was, indeed, waiting, and looked very beautiful in a cloud of white satin and lace.

'She was lost in admiration of herself in the mirror,' Aunt Helen explained.

'I'm not surprised. You look very lovely,' Jodi said generously. Then, when Skye didn't speak, 'Well? How do I look?'

Skye put her head on one side, giving Jodi her complete attention, trying to put everything else out of her mind. 'You look young—and beautiful and—and virginal,' she offered.

Both Jodi and her aunt looked taken aback for a moment at that last adjective, but then Jodi said practically, 'How does it fit?'

'Oh! OK, I suppose. It feels all right.' Belatedly Skye remembered why they were here, and held out her arms so that they could see.

Aunt Helen went round her, examining every seam, and then pronounced herself satisfied. 'Yes, they've done a very good job. And Jodi is still the same weight, thank goodness.'

'That's hardly surprising, after the way you've been nagging me not to eat too little or too much these last few weeks,' Jodi said in laughing happiness.

'Now what about your hair, Skye?' Aunt Helen murmured. 'Perhaps it might look better up.'

She began to experiment with styles while Skye stood patiently, letting them do what they wanted. She still felt numb and longed to be on her own, but that chance didn't come until much later that day, because after they'd left the fashion house she had to go with them to help Jodi choose some more clothes for her trousseau, and after lunch they did some more sightseeing, so they didn't get back to the apartment until early evening.

While they were shopping Skye had again asked Jodi what she would like for a wedding present, but her cousin was still undecided. 'I'll let you know before we go back to Nassau,' was the only promise Skye could get from her, and one which was pretty useless as she intended to take off the next morning. She also wanted to give Aunt Helen a present, but couldn't think of anything her aunt didn't already have in abundance. Then she remembered the sketch of Jodi. At one point Skye had toyed with the idea of giving it to Thane, but, remembering how lonely her aunt had said she would be once

Jodi was married, Skye decided that Aunt Helen might like it more. Not that it was much of a present, but she had put quite a lot of time into it, and perhaps it might help a little when she told them that she was leaving in the morning.

While Jodi was changing for dinner in the bathroom, Skye put the finishing touches to the sketch and then changed herself. She had intended to tell them while they were having dinner, but when she came into the main room found that Thane had arrived and brought Angie with him.

'Hi. I thought I might as well bring those books over for you myself,' Angie greeted her.

'Why, how kind of you.' Skye took the books and glanced at the titles. 'They look most exciting. Thank you.'

'And they're having an exhibition of one of those artist's works at a Manhattan gallery, with a special viewing tonight,' Angie added. 'I got a couple of tickets and wondered if you'd come along with me?'

'Why, thank you. I should like to very much.' Skye accepted unhesitatingly, grateful for Angie's thoughtfulness and glad to get away from the apartment for the evening.

Thane and Angie stayed to dinner, but just before the two girls left for the art exhibition Skye remembered the present for her aunt and gave her the sketch of Jodi. 'Just to say thank you for having me to stay,' she murmured quietly as she kissed her aunt's cheek.

'Oh, what a marvellous present. John, do come and look at this drawing of Jodi that Skye has given me.'

Skye had intended to slip away, but that was impossible now. Everyone wanted to look at the drawing and comment, Jodi most of all. Then an idea hit her and she turned to Skye. 'You once said you sometimes did proper portraits; did you mean in oils?'

'Well, I have done, yes, but they take such a lot of time that...'

But her cousin interrupted excitedly. 'Then that's what I want. For a wedding present. I want you to paint a portrait of Thane for me.'

Skye's face paled as she stared at Jodi in consternation. 'Oh, but I couldn't! It's impossible.'

'Don't be so modest, dear,' Aunt Helen joined in. 'I'm quite sure you'd paint a marvellous picture. I think it's a wonderful idea.'

'No, please.' Skye tried desperately to persuade them, terrified at the thought of spending so many hours alone with Thane. 'You don't understand. A portrait isn't like a sketch. It takes a long time. At least two weeks, possibly more. And lots of sittings. And you're—we're going back to Nassau in a few days.'

'But you could stay on here in New York,' Jodi suggested, resolved now to have her way. 'You could use this room as a studio, and Thane could come round in the evenings to sit for you. Couldn't you, darling?' she appealed to Thane. 'Don't you think that's a good idea?'

But before he could answer Skye said quickly, 'That's still no good. I didn't bring any oils or a big enough easel with me. I'm sorry. I'll—I'll do a sketch of him, if you like.'

But Jodi was stubbornly determined to have her portrait. 'You can easily go out and buy what you need. There must be dozens of art suppliers in New York. Angie would know. She'll help you.'

'Why, yes, of course,' Angie agreed, almost as eagerly as Jodi. 'I'll be happy to.'

'But it's impossible,' Skye repeated. She had carefully kept her eyes away from Thane, but now she turned in his direction, although she couldn't meet his eyes. 'And you haven't asked Thane how he feels about it; he's so busy, maybe he doesn't want to waste hours sitting for his portrait.'

There had been a note of pleading in her voice, and Skye could only hope that Thane would understand and rescue her. Slowly, uncertainly, she raised her eyes to meet his and found him watching her, a strange, almost pensive frown between his brows.

'It won't be a waste of time! Of course you'll sit, won't you, darling?' Jodi pressed him.

He gave her a reflective look. 'Skye is here on vacation, Jodi. You can't ask her to spend her time working on a portrait.'

'Oh, but it's only painting! That isn't work. And besides, she did that picture for Daddy.' Jodi's voice became petulant. 'I don't know what all the fuss is about. You did ask me what I wanted, Skye.'

'Yes, I know, but I . . .'

'If you're worried about staying behind in New York, you needn't be,' Uncle John said. 'I'll be here at the apartment as well, you know.'

'There,' Jodi said with satisfaction. 'And you will sit, won't you, Thane? I should so love to have your portrait to put on the wall in our new apartment.'

Thane didn't an_ across at Skye's pale _ remembering that kiss in_ a little, and she felt a grea_. His jaw hardened he was going to refuse. Sh_ of relief because turning her head away as he b_ped her eyes, course I'll sit for it,' he added, to speak. 'Of brought Skye's eyes rushing back to _ face, 'But perhaps Skye just doesn't want to paint _ picture.'

There was the slightest inflexion on the _ny' that made Skye's heart start to whirl. She stood very still, her thoughts chaotic, trying to make common sense conquer emotion, but failing completely. So it was her heart that answered when she said unsteadily, 'Of course I—I want to paint you.'

Thane's chin lifted a little, but his eyes still held hers as he said, 'Good, that's settled, then.'

THE REST of that week seemed to pass in a bemused haze that only lifted when Skye went with Angie in the latter's lunchbreak to one of the best art suppliers in the city. There she bought oils and canvas, brushes and easel, and all the other things she needed before she could even begin to paint. She tried very hard to push her feelings for Thane out of her mind, but to deny her love for him was like denying one's arm or leg: it was there for life and that was it.

Luckily Thane had to go over to Washington on a case for a few days, and didn't return until the Friday. The Bentons stayed over in New York for the weekend instead of going back to Nassau, and Jodi eagerly demanded to know when Skye would start the picture, as if she just had to stand in front of the easel and get on with it.

'It isn't that simple,' Skye protested. 'I have to do a lot of preliminary work first.'

Uncle John had a really good camera with a close-up lens which Skye borrowed to take lots of photographs of Thane. Most of the shots were just head and shoulders, a few full length, although she had already more or less decided on the size of the painting because of the time restriction. But there were different backgrounds and lights to try out, and she had to choose from which side she was going to paint him, whether it was to be life-size or smaller. Thane was very patient, moving to wherever she asked and turning his head as she instructed him, a faint glint sometimes coming into his eyes when she moved forward as if to put him into a pose, then hastily stopped and tried to describe what she wanted instead.

The films were taken to be developed, and were ready for collection within twenty-four hours. Skye pored over them, trying to decide what position to use and not feeling particularly happy with any of them. They just weren't right, somehow. Thane came in for some ribbing from Scott, who said that it was no wonder Skye was having such a hard time making up her mind when she had such an ugly subject.

On Saturday afternoon Scott called in to say that some friends had passed on four tickets to a Broadway show for him because they were unable to go at the last minute. Would Jodi and Skye like to go as a foursome with him and Thane? As the tickets for that particular show were like gold dust, Jodi agreed at once. He called to pick them up with Thane beside him, but said, 'I've got to call at a hotel to pick up the tickets from my friends first.'

Skye sat in the back with Jodi, her eyes on the back of Thane's head, still wondering how she would paint him, and hardly noticed when they drew up outside the portico of the hotel. Glancing at his watch, Scott said, 'We're early; we may as well have a drink while we're here.' And immediately he got out of the car and held the door for Skye. They followed him into the hotel quite unsuspectingly—and walked straight into a surprise party for Thane!

Nearly everyone there was a friend of his, either from college, law school or his law firm, plus some wives and girlfriends. For a moment Thane looked completely taken aback, his face grim, as if he wouldn't have chosen this, but then he forced a smile and began to shake hands with everyone as they pressed forward to say hello. Perhaps he was the type who didn't like surprises, Skye thought. But Jodi, of course, was loving every minute. She stood beside Thane, sparkling and happy, shaking hands eagerly as each person was introduced, completely in her element. Skye watched them, realising this was a foretaste of what the wedding reception would be like in just a few weeks' time, then turned away, her eyes desolate.

'Hello, Skye.' She found that Angie was standing beside her and watching her curiously. 'Quite a surprise, wasn't it? Sorry we couldn't let you into the secret, but we didn't want Jodi to know.'

'Afraid she might have let the cat out of the bag?' Skye said with a smile.

'Well, we didn't think she'd *say* anything, but we knew that she wouldn't be able to resist dressing up for a party, so that Thane would have been bound to suspect something.' She glanced across at her brother. 'Not that he seemed altogether delighted at first, did he?'

'Perhaps he was overcome by the surprise,' Skye answered lightly, wondering whether Angie liked Jodi.

'Perhaps.' Angie turned to Skye. 'Have you decided how you're going to paint him yet?'

Skye gave a rueful shake of her head. 'Not yet, I'm afraid. I'm just hoping an idea will come.'

Scott came up then with drinks for them both, introduced Skye to some people standing near her and took Angie off with him to see about the food.

It was a very informal party, mostly everyone stood around eating and drinking, but as time went on several began to dance. Skye met a lot of people, all of them fascinated by her soft British accent, as well as her fragile beauty. She smiled and laughed like everyone else and tried very hard to enjoy herself. She danced once with Scott, but noticed that he spent most of his time with Angie, who acted as hostess at the party. Thane and Jodi always seemed to be lost among his friends, although Skye often heard Jodi's excited laugh above the hubbub of noise and conversation.

A man Skye had been moving around the floor with—you could hardly call it dancing—went to get her another drink and she walked to a quieter corner of the room, feeling hot despite the efficient air-conditioning. She felt strangely detached from the rest of the party. But then she was a stranger, a foreigner. It seemed funny to think of herself as that, especially when everyone had been so friendly and welcoming. Soon she would leave here and never come back. A great sadness filled her heart, and Skye looked across the room to where she could see Thane's fair head among a group of other men. Almost as if she'd called his name, he raised his head and turned until their eyes met. Their glances held for a few seconds and then Thane spoke to the people near him, edged his way through the group and came straight over to her. 'Hi,' he said in a strange, husky kind of voice.

'Hello. Are you—are you enjoying your party?'

'I'm enjoying meeting my friends again,' he said obliquely. 'But the occasion—that's something else.'

Skye looked at him, not understanding, but not caring very much. She remembered another time when she and he had stood alone under the shade of a flame tree, and she suddenly knew how she would paint him. Her face broke into a smile that transformed her face, and Thane caught his breath, an arrested look in his blue eyes. 'What is it?'

'I can see now how I must paint you. I suddenly remem—— It suddenly came to me.'

'Not here,' he said quickly. 'Not in a place like this, at a party like this.'

'Oh, no! No,' she hastened to reassure him, then smiled. 'You'll see—when it's finished.'

'Aren't you going to let me see it till then?'

'It might be a failure.'

'Then you'll just have to paint another.'

There was some insinuation in his voice, something in the way he looked at her that made Skye's throat tighten so much that she couldn't speak. All she could do was shake her head and look away, her feelings raw.

'Skye.' There was a sudden urgency in Thane's voice as he said, 'I have to talk to you. I——'

He broke off as Jodi came up to them. 'Hi. Isn't this a great party?' she enthused. 'You OK, Skye? Who are that couple over by the bar? I haven't met them yet.' And she pulled Thane away to introduce her.

The weekend over, Aunt Helen and Jodi flew back to Nassau on Monday morning to go on with the wedding arrangements. Uncle John drove them to the airport and went on to his own office, leaving

Skye alone in the apartment. The cleaning and housework had already been done by a cleaning service who sent someone round twice a week, so Skye had nothing to do but her own work and to prepare the portrait of Thane for when he came for his first sitting that evening. Her own work she got through quite quickly, then she parcelled it up and walked along the block till she found a post office where she could send it off to England, together with a letter to her parents. It was still very hot, the sun directly overhead so that even the sky-scrapers didn't provide any shade. Lured by the thought of a shady tree, Skye ventured into Central Park, bought herself a hamburger and a Coke and sat down on a bench to watch the world go by, amazed that people were actually jogging and playing ball games in the heat.

It was a relief to get back to the apartment and take a cold shower. Afterwards Skye got out the photographs of Thane again and pinned a couple to the top left-hand corner of the easel, then placed some paper on it and began to do some preliminary drawings from the photographs. It was going to be very hard to do this painting, she knew that. Not from an artistic point of view—as a professional she couldn't do anything but her best work—but from the emotional angle it was going to be terribly difficult. Somehow she had to try and hide feelings that she was all too afraid Thane was already aware of. She would have to get through the hours of being alone with him, finding safe subjects to talk about and keeping her mind on her work.

But they wouldn't be entirely alone, she remembered. Uncle John would be here in the evenings, so he and Thane could talk to each other. And, if by any chance Uncle John left them alone, why she could—she could play some classical music very loudly, Skye decided. Wagner, or something like that. Making up her mind to sort out some records so that she would have them ready, Skye went over to the shelves to see what she could find, but a few minutes later laughed to herself as she realised that the Bentons' taste didn't run to that kind of music. The nearest thing to classical music was Gershwin, but after a moment's reflection she decided that would be more than adequate.

The doorbell rang and, still smiling a little, Skye went to answer it. It was Thane. He was leaning against the door-jamb, dressed in a lightweight business suit, but with the jacket slung over his shoulder, his tie loose, 'Hi.' He straightened up and walked in, then turned to watch Skye as she closed the door. 'You haven't put the chain on.'

'Oh, no, I forgot.'

'And you didn't look through the spyhole before you opened the door. If you're going to be alone here during the day, then you'll have to be security-minded.'

Sensing that he was in a strange mood, Skye nodded. 'I'll try and remember. It's just that we don't have any of those things at home.' She crossed to the bar. 'Would you like a drink? How about teaching me to make a cocktail? What shall we have—a vodka martini shaken but not stirred? Or how about a Manhattan?'

Thane looked at her for a moment and then his mouth quirked into a grin. Dropping his jacket on to a chair, he pushed his thick hair back from his face and came to join her. 'I have one that's perfect for an English girl like you; it's called Foggy Day.'

Skye wrinkled her nose at him. 'In that case, I shall make you an Americano.'

They finished mixing the drinks around the same time and formally presented them to each other. 'What shall we drink to?' Thane wanted to know.

Skye looked down into her drink, trying to think of something suitable, but she was intensely aware of his nearness, of the heated masculine smell of him, of his strength, of everything about him. 'Why, to the future, of course,' she said rather sharply. 'To yours and Jodi's.'

Thane gave a short, almost bitter laugh. 'I have a better idea; let's drink to the success of the picture.'

He clinked his glass against hers and Skye took a long drink, then gasped. 'Good heavens! What did you put in this? It's very strong.'

'Yeah, well, maybe we need something strong.' Thane finished his own cocktail and put down the glass. 'Mind if I take a shower?'

'No, of course not. You can use Uncle John's room; he isn't home yet.'

'No, I guess it's too early for him.' He left her to slowly finish her drink, and when he came back he had changed into a clean shirt from his briefcase.

'You came prepared,' Skye said lightly.

'Mm.' He came to stand beside her and look at the photograph she'd pinned to the easel, and now he smelt of soap and sharp, tangy aftershave. 'Is this what you're going to do?' He touched the photo with a long finger.

'Yes, I think so. But I'd like to do some preliminary sketches first, if you don't mind. Shall we start?'

He hesitated, but then shrugged. 'Go ahead.' Thane moved over to the chair Skye had placed in a corner of the room against a blank wall. 'Like this?'

'Yes, that's fine. But if you could turn your head slightly more to the left. That's great.'

Skye began to draw quickly, and was soon so absorbed in what she was doing that she jumped when the doorbell rang again. 'Oh, that will be Uncle John.' She ran to open the door, only remembering to look through the hole when Thane called out to remind her. 'It's OK. It is him.'

'Hello. Have you started already?' Uncle John came in hot and tired and immediately went to shower. When he came back, they all had another drink and then ate the meal Skye had made earlier.

'This is a pleasant surprise,' Uncle John remarked. 'I would have sent out for something, you know.'

'I had all afternoon,' Skye said lightly.

'It's delicious. I should warn you, Thane, that Jodi's cooking isn't a patch on this,' her uncle joked.

After dinner, Skye spent another hour on the sketches. Uncle John stayed in the room, but presently fell asleep in front of the television set, only waking when Thane left.

During the following days Skye went out to art galleries and twice met Angie for lunch, but that evening set a pattern for the next few nights. Thane came to the apartment first and they experimented with new cocktails, with Skye always keeping things light and informal on the surface until she could relax when Uncle John came home and they had dinner. But on Friday, early in the afternoon, Uncle John rang to say that a meeting he'd set up had to be cancelled and he'd decided to fly down to Nassau straight away, instead of on Saturday morning as he'd intended. So when Skye went to answer Thane's ring it was with the knowledge that they would be alone all that evening.

'Hi.' He came in and dumped his jacket as usual. 'I've got a good cocktail for you tonight.'

'I've already made yours. Try it. Bet you can't guess what it is.'

She watched as he tasted the drink she'd poured from the electric shaker. 'It's a Southern Sour,' he guessed.

'Close. It's a Scarlett O'Hara.' She paused, then said, 'Uncle John won't be here tonight. He's gone straight to Nassau.'

'I know. He called me. He asked me to get Angie to come and stay here with you so you wouldn't be alone.'

Slowly Skye lifted her eyes to looked at him. 'And is she coming?'

'No.' He shook his head and gave her the drink he'd been working on. 'Here, try it.'

Skye took a sip. 'Why isn't she coming?'

'Because I never asked her. I thought maybe you'd like to go and stay at my parents' place instead. Well, what do you think of the drink?' he demanded before Skye could think of anything to say.

'I like it. What's it called?'

'Golden Dream,' he told her, his voice soft. 'Well, will you come?'

'Thank you. It's very kind of your parents to invite me. Angie will be there, will she?'

'We'll all be there.'

Her eyes widening, Skye said, 'You too? Aren't you going down to Nassau tomorrow to be with Jodi?'

He shook his head decisively. 'No, I figured it was about time I had a weekend at home. And I also figured it was about time I took you out to dinner, so I'll give you twenty minutes to change. OK?'

'But what about the picture?' Skye called after him as he made for Uncle John's room and the shower.

He turned at the door and grinned at her. 'There'll be time.'

That evening was the most wonderful in Skye's life. Thane not only gave her dinner, but he showed her the New Yorker's New York. It was still light at first, and Thane drove her down to the waterfront where they took a boat round the harbour and he pointed out Ellis Island where all the European settlers had first arrived. He told her poignant stories of the hundreds who had been turned away, and was amazed to see her eyes fill with tears. 'Sorry,' she apologised. 'I'm a sucker for a sad story.'

They went up in the lift inside the Statue of Liberty and looked out at the most awe-inspiring manmade landscape in the world—and it seemed only natural that Thane should put his hand on her shoulder as he pointed out all the landmarks. It

grew darker and they stayed to watch as the lights
gradually came on, turning what had been majestic
and impressive into a glittering wonderland. When
they got hungry they ate: a hot dog from one stall,
pretzels dipped in mustard from another, washed
down by a beer from a bar in what had once been
a speakeasy. Thane bought her a silly souvenir of
an Uncle Sam doll, and Skye laughed but determined to keep it forever.

They walked, rode on boats and buses, listened
to jazz in a cave of gloom, watched the sunset reflected in a million windows, gave money to some
street musicians, looked at statues, explored
Chinatown. So many sights, so many new sen-
sations, that they all became a blur in Skye's
memory, like watching a lot of colour slides that
had got out of order. But they were all pivoted to
the centre point, to Thane, and being out alone with
him for the first and possibly the only time.

It was already late when he took Skye back to
the apartment to pack some clothes, but the roads
were clear now as they drove out of New York and
crossed the river to go to Thane's home. A welcoming light shone out from the porch of the old,
timber-framed building when Thane drew up in the
driveway, but otherwise the house was in darkness.
Thane unlocked the door and they went in quietly,
then tiptoed up the stairs, making Skye feel like a
schoolgirl again. The moon was very bright and
there was light enough to s   but Thane took her
arm as he led Skye across the landing to where a
door stood open. 'This is your room,' he said in
an undertone. 'The bathroom is next door. And
Angie is on your other side. I'm down the hall.'

'OK. Thanks.' She turned to go in, then called softly, 'Thane?'

'Yes.' He was instantly back, his face intent.

'Just, thank you. For—for tonight.'

He nodded and seemed about to say something, but Skye grew suddenly afraid and went quickly into her room.

It was strange to wake up to the sound of birdsong again, almost like being back home. The room was very pretty. Skye sat up and looked round approvingly. Old colonial furniture that looked original, an exquisitely worked patchwork quilt, and lots of pictures on plain walls. Yes, definitely like home. And Thane's parents and Angie were so welcoming that they immediately made her feel at ease, too.

Life was lived at a much slower pace here than at Nassau; there was no immediate organisation of time so that you could cram as much activity as possible into the weekend. Skye went with Angie to the local centre they called the village, and found it not unlike an English country town, with a wide, tree-lined main street, bow-fronted antique shops and graceful buildings. They spent a couple of contented hours browsing round the shops, and came back to the house to find Thane stripped to the waist while he helped his father to stack a load of logs that had just been delivered.

Mrs Tyson was a keen gardener, so the gardens around the house were very beautiful and she loved to show them off. In Skye she found another lover of nature, and they spent the afternoon wandering around it together and ended up in the greenhouse, happily repotting plants. Dinner was the main meal

of the day and went on far into the evening,
everyone having opinions on every subject that
came up, and not afraid to put them eloquently and
forcefully. To Skye, it was just like mealtime back
in England, and she joined in quite naturally,
finding it stimulating after the social chit-chat that
was usual in Nassau.

On Sunday morning they all went to church, and
lunch afterwards was another meal with talk being
more important than the food. Only there were
other guests to this meal, Scott being one of them.
After lunch everyone went out into the garden, but
after a while Skye wandered inside and sat down
at the piano. The two days she had spent here had
been so happy; she felt a small feeling of loneliness
knowing that tomorrow morning she would be
leaving. Lifting the lid of the piano, she began to
play softly. Coming from a musical family, she had
been taught to play from the moment her pudgy
baby fingers had had the strength to pick out a note,
her parents hoping that she would be a child
prodigy, or at least follow in their footsteps. She
had done neither, of course, but was still a far above
average player.

'That's a sad tune.' Thane had come in and was
standing by the piano, watching her.

She gave a ghost of a smile and switched to a
jazz number. 'How about this?'

He shook his head and sat down beside her. 'Do
you know this one?'

The haunting tune of 'Cavatina' filled the room.
Skye nodded, and after a few moments began to
join in. They didn't speak until the piece was fin-

ished, the notes slowly dying away into the gathering dusk.

'Why are you called Skye?' Thane said at length.

'It's the name of an island off the coast of Scotland. My parents went there for a holiday once and fell in love with it. It's very beautiful, with soft blue-grey skies and waves rippling on the shore. And in the spring all the fields and hills are full of flowers.'

'Then you're like your name,' Thane said, his eyes on her face. 'Everything about you is soft: your hair, your eyes, your skin, your lips.' His voice slowed as he lingered on her mouth. 'I should like to go to Skye, to see it for myself.'

'Maybe you will. When—when you're with Jodi, on your honeym——'

Her words were stilled as Thane suddenly put out a hand and covered hers. 'Don't say that!' he said with fierce intensity. 'Don't ever say it again.'

She stared at him wide-eyed. 'But, Thane, I...'

'We have to talk, Skye,' he interrupted urgently. 'Everything is changed; you know that.'

'No!' Skye got agitatedly to her feet. 'Please don't. I...'

'Why have you stopped playing? The music sounded so lovely outside.' Mrs Tyson had come into the room behind them. 'You play extremely well, Skye. Won't you go on?'

'If—if you like.' She hesitated, but Thane got up from the stool and went to sit in a chair across the room. Skye began to play again, but livelier tunes this time as the others started to drift in from the garden. Angie had a good voice and began to sing, and soon everyone was joining in. After a while

Mrs Tyson took over at the piano, and Skye went to sit in the deep window-seat where the scents from the garden drifted through the open windows.

Presently, as she had been afraid he would, Thane came casually over to stand beside her, carrying two glasses of wine. 'You must be thirsty,' he remarked, handing her a glass.

'Thanks.' She didn't look at him, instead keeping her eyes fixed on the piano where Angie and Scott were now trying to play a duet, not with much success but with a great deal of laughter.

'Why don't we take a walk in the garden?' Thane suggested quietly. 'We can't talk in here.'

But Skye said, 'Angie told me that she has started seeing Scott *again*. Did they go out together in the past?'

'Yes. A few years ago. Skye, please, I have to...'

'What happened?' she interrupted quickly.

Thane sighed and ran his hand through his hair again. 'Angie didn't want to commit herself. She was enjoying her independence too much.' Realising that Skye wouldn't walk in the garden with him, he sat down on the seat beside her, necessarily close. Skye's heart began to beat painfully, and the hand that held her drink trembled so that she had to put the drink down on a table beside her.

'Skye, you're a very honest person,' Thane said softly under cover of the music. 'So please don't try to pretend that nothing has happened.'

'Nothing has,' she insisted, refusing to look at him.

'Hasn't it?' He reached out and put his hand over hers where it lay on the seat between them. At his unexpected touch she gasped, and a great shudder of awareness ran through her. 'Hasn't it?' Thane repeated, his grip tightening.

'No.' The word was torn from her as she turned to look at him, at his face gazing so intently into her own. 'Nothing must change. Not ever!' And she quickly drew her hand away and went over to stand with the group around the piano.

With so many people there it was easy enough to avoid being alone with Thane for the rest of the evening, but when Skye went to bed that night it was impossible to sleep. Her heart was filled with a crazy kind of excitement, coupled with a great feeling of guilt. And perhaps the guilt was made heavier because she had been made so welcome and had enjoyed herself so much in Thane's home. For two days she had seen what it would be like to be Jodi, to come here as Thane's fiancée—or even his wife. But if she'd been his wife they wouldn't be separated by the length of the house as they were now, they would be held close in each other's arms, making love in the big old-fashioned bed.

Her body on fire with sudden heat, Skye pushed aside such useless, impossible thoughts and got out of bed. The window was open and she leaned out, letting what little breeze there was cool her heated skin. There was a light in one of the bedrooms further along, casting a bright square in the garden below. As she watched, a shadow entered the square, filled it, then turned and moved away. It was Thane, she realised, pacing the floor in his room, finding it as impossible to sleep as she.

In the morning, after an early breakfast, Skye drove back to New York with Angie and Thane, and asked Thane to drop her off at one of the shopping malls near the apartment. He did so, but quickly got out of the car to open the door for her. 'I'll see you at the apartment this evening,' he said urgently. 'I'll be there as early as I can.' Perhaps he read fear in her eyes, because he put a hand on her arm. 'Be there—*please*.'

Skye bit her lip, then nodded. 'Yes. All—all right.'

She watched them drive away, then went into the mall to find a music shop. To her delight they had a copy of the record she wanted: her mother playing a solo of a piece of music that her father had composed and arranged specially for her. The shop assistant was very helpful, and promised to have it wrapped and sent as a thank-you gift to Thane's parents. That done, Skye went on to the apartment where she meant to work on Thane's portrait, but instead of working she stood gazing at it, her thoughts in turmoil. At the moment the picture was still very much in the embryo stage. The outline drawing was there, and she had painted in some of his hair to get the shape of his face, and his shoulders. It was coming along well, all things considered. Another week should do it, Skye decided, and grew afraid again. Afraid of what he might ask of her. Afraid, because there was only one answer, and soon she would never see him again. Raising her fingers to gently touch the picture, Skye realised that soon this would be gone, too. But then an idea struck her and she gave a sudden smile. Snatching up her bag, she ran out of the apartment, hailed a cab and told the driver to take her to the art suppliers again.

From about four that afternoon Skye was a bag of nerves as she waited for Thane to come, but he must have got held up because it was her uncle who came home first. He was full of the weekend in Nassau, and told it all over again when Thane finally arrived about six. Uncle John had lots of messages from Jodi to Thane, mostly about wedding presents that had arrived while they were away, or progress with the arrangements for the ceremony. He went on talking even after Skye had started to paint, but presently went into his den on the other side of the hall to make some phone calls.

As soon as he was gone, Thane said, 'We must meet somewhere.'

'No, Thane, we can't. There's really nothing we have to...'

'Will you meet me for lunch tomorrow?'

'No! I can't possibly. Oh!' She found that she'd put some paint in the wrong place and had to scrape it off.

'OK, then, I'll come here.'

'*No*, that's even worse.' Skye stepped from behind the easel in distress, and Thane suddenly smiled. 'What is it?' she asked in bewilderment.

'You have a dab of paint on your nose.' His voice softened. 'And you look very beautiful.'

'Oh, Thane.' She stood looking at him, her eyes revealing everything she had been trying so hard to hide.

One look at her face brought him swiftly to his feet and across the room. Taking her hand, he said urgently, 'Please, Skye. Just meet me tomorrow so that we can talk. We have to sort this out.'

'No, it wouldn't do any good.'

'How can you be sure? Don't you think we owe it to ourselves—and to Jodi—to try?'

She shook her head in indecision, her hand trembling agitatedly in his. But then she heard Uncle John start to come back and said, 'I—oh, yes, then. Where?'

'I'll call you tomorrow morning.'

Quickly Thane went back to his seat and Skye returned to the easel, but her hands were shaking so much that she could hardly hold the brush, and very little more work got done that evening.

Thane called at about ten the next morning and asked Skye to meet him in the café in the Fountain Court inside the Metropolitan Museum of Art at twelve-thirty. Unable to settle to anything, she got ready early, putting on a cool, pale orange dress and matching sandals that she'd bought here in New York, then took a cab to Fifth Avenue and wandered around a department store until it was time to meet Thane. Reluctantly, then, she walked to the museum, but it took a while for her to make up her mind to walk into the café to meet him.

He had been watching the door, and stood up at once when she came in. She went to his table and Thane put a hand on her arm, as if he was afraid she might turn and run away.

'I was beginning to be afraid you wouldn't come.'

'I almost didn't,' she admitted. 'Thane, I really don't think...'

'Sit down. Would you like something to eat? A drink, then?' when she shook her head.

'Please. Something long and cool.'

He ordered and suddenly seemed uncertain himself. 'I have so much I want to say to you, but

I—I hardly know where to begin. I suppose all there
is to say, really, is that I've realised that getting engaged to Jodi was the biggest mistake of my life.
And that has to be put right before it's too late.'
He reached out to take Skye's hand, and looked at
her earnestly. 'And that meeting you has been the
luckiest thing that ever happened to me. Skye, I
want...'

But she quickly raised her free hand and put it
against his lips. 'Don't. Don't say any more. Jodi
is my cousin. I can't—I can't hurt her. I won't come
between you.'

Reaching up, Thane took hold of her wrist, then
deliberately kissed her palm. 'It's too late, Skye.
There's no way I can marry Jodi now.'

'But you must,' Skye said in distress. 'The
wedding—it's only a few weeks away.'

'It wouldn't work,' he said urgently. 'Surely you
can see that?' He pushed his hair back with a
harassed hand. 'Maybe it was a mistake from the
start. I don't know how much you know, but Jodi
used to go with Scott, and at the time I was going
pretty steady with another girl. Well, about the time
this girl and I broke up, Scott dropped Jodi and...'

'*Scott* dropped Jodi?' Skye asked, remembering
that Jodi's version had been just the opposite.

'That's right. Well, I was pretty fed up, and I
guess Jodi was too. We kind of hit each other on
the rebound, and in next to no time we were suddenly engaged to be married and the wedding arrangements were in hand.' He ran a hand over his
chin. 'It was my fault, I should have made her hold
back, but right then there didn't seem to be much

left in life except ambition, and Jodi fed that. She's
the right kind of wife for an ambitious man.'

Turning his head to look directly at her, Thane
went on, 'And to be honest, if you hadn't come
along I would probably have married her and we
might have muddled through—just so long as I'd
gone on being ambitious and successful. But when
I got to know you . . . No, let me finish,' he insisted
when Skye started to protest. 'When you came
along, it made me realise just how superficial Jodi
is. There's no depth to her character, no strengths,
no deep emotions. But you . . . Skye, please don't
turn away. A man could love you—and be content
with just loving you for the rest of his life.'

Tears came to her eyes, and Skye tried hard to
blink them away. 'Oh, hell! Did you have to say
that to me when all these people are around?'

Thane gave a crooked smile, his eyes intent on
her face. 'Well, I know you're a sucker for a sob
story.' But then his hands tightened on hers as he
held it between his own. 'I'm in love with you, Skye.
I want to spend the rest of my life taking care of
you. No other woman has ever made me feel like
that.'

His words should have filled her with happiness,
and in a way they did, because she loved him so
much, but it also felt terribly wrong. How could
they possibly find happiness together if it meant
destroying someone else's life? Hardening her heart
for what she knew she had to do, Skye said shortly,
'Oh, really? And what makes you think you won't
change your mind again when some other girl comes
along?'

Thane's mouth tightened. 'I've already explained about Jodi. This time I'm sure of how I feel about you. You want to know why? Because I did what you're doing; I tried to fight it. I told myself it was all wrong, that I couldn't possibly be falling in love with you when I was engaged to Jodi. But it didn't work; the more I tried to fight it, the more deeply I fell for you. And then that night in the pool...'

'When you kissed me because you thought I was Jodi,' Skye interrupted firmly.

'Only for a few seconds—then I knew it was you. After that, I couldn't get you out of my mind. I wanted to kiss you again, and I wanted to be honest with you as you'd been honest with me.'

'It was just an experiment,' Skye lied as convincingly as she could. 'I just wondered what you were like to kiss, that's all. Why should I pretend I thought you were Scott when it didn't mean anything?'

'I don't believe that,' Thane said sharply. He reached out for her hand, but she moved it quickly to her lap and he gave a short laugh. 'You're afraid to even let me touch you in case you give yourself away. But it doesn't matter. I know you care about me. You're too open and vulnerable to be able to hide it. So please don't pretend, Skye. Not any more. This means too much.'

Biting her lip, Skye looked down at the table, close to tears. 'It would be better if you tried to believe me,' she said huskily. She looked up, her eyes overbright. 'Don't you see? Jodi is my cousin, part of my family. If you gave her up for me, the result would be—be appalling. I'd be accused of breaking you up and there'd be a terrible row. And it would be true—you said yourself you would have gone ahead and married Jodi if I hadn't come along. I couldn't be responsible for that.'

'You're not—*I* am,' Thane retorted urgently. 'I know that it isn't going to be pleasant for either of us, but don't you realise that it's surely better to end it now?' His voice suddenly became harsh. 'What do you want me to do—marry a woman I don't love just to save a family row?'

Colour heightened Skye's cheeks. 'Have you thought of what you're doing to Jodi? She loves you. She...'

'Does she?' Thane's mouth twisted. 'I'm sure as hell beginning to doubt it. She would have married Scott if he'd asked her. Now I wonder if she isn't marrying me just to spite him.'

'Oh, no!' Skye stared at him in horror. 'She wouldn't do that.'

'No? What's the betting when I tell her it's all off she doesn't turn to Scott again?'

'Please don't say any more. It just doesn't make any difference, can't you see that? There can never be anything between us.'

Agitatedly she got to her feet, but Thane caught her arm before she could walk away. His grip hurting, he looked into her face and said earnestly, 'I'm going down to Nassau at the weekend to tell Jodi that we're through. No matter what happens between you and me, nothing can change the fact that the wedding is off.'

'You can't be so cruel,' Skye pleaded, knowing how she would feel if it happened to her.

'I *have* to be!' His gaze devoured her. 'Skye, it's you I love. I want you so much. And I know you love me.'

She stared back at him for a moment, her eyes wet with unshed tears, then she shook her head in denial and, pulling her arm free, she turned and ran from him, threading her way through the crowded café until she was lost from sight.

CHAPTER SEVEN

Skye half hoped that Thane wouldn't come to the apartment to sit for his portrait that evening, but he did, arriving shortly after Uncle John, his mouth drawn into a tense, tight line. He had obviously hoped to arrive before her uncle but, seeing he was there, Thane just said he couldn't stay too long and she began to paint at once.

He was a difficult subject tonight: there were storm clouds in his eyes as he looked at her, and his jaw was set in an angry thrust of determination. Of necessity, their eyes often met and tension built, a tautness so electric that Skye was sure her uncle would sense it. But he sat placidly at his desk, working on some business papers, seemingly unaware of the atmosphere around him.

Usually they talked as she worked, but tonight they were silent as Skye tried hard to concentrate on the painting. Strangely, she worked well, perhaps lit by the fire in Thane's eyes as she tried to capture his mood of anger and determination. The picture gradually came to life under her hands, just Thane's head and shoulders against a dark background, captured in this moment of tension when his face was taut and alive with emotion.

The time flew past, but after nearly two hours Thane stood up abruptly. 'I've got to go.' He came towards her. 'How's it going? When do I get to see it?'

'Not yet.' She put out a protective arm to keep him away. 'When it's finished. After—after Jodi's seen it.'

Thane looked at her for a moment, his jaw clenched, then turned to say goodnight to Uncle John. There was awkwardness in his manner as he did so, and Skye guessed how much it must embarrass him to come here when he no longer wanted to marry Jodi. Turning to Skye he said softly, 'I'll call you tomorrow.'

She began to shake her head, but became still when she saw the way Thane looked at her, his feelings clear to read. Skye would have given a great deal to be able to walk into his arms and be held and kissed, but they weren't alone and she could only say 'Goodnight, Thane,' in a strained voice and close the door behind him.

Sleep didn't come until very late that night. Skye lay in bed, listening to the gentle whirr of the air-conditioning, trying to work out what she ought to do. It seemed that her attempt at trying to make Thane believe that she didn't care about him just wasn't going to work. He wasn't a fool; he knew the effect he had on her. And it looked as though nothing was going to stop him from breaking his engagement to Jodi. He would be free then. For a few moments Skye indulged in a wonderful dream of what that could mean, but she suddenly felt scared, wondering if true and lasting happiness could ever be attained when it was based on hurt done to others. Because it wouldn't only be Jodi who was hurt, but her aunt and uncle, too. They would rightly feel that she had betrayed their hospitality and would probably never speak to her again.

But it was Jodi who Skye was most concerned for. She knew what it was to be in love with Thane, and her heart recoiled in terror at the thought of what losing him might be like. It would be a blow that Jodi might never recover from. And she was a creature of moods; if she got depressed and hysterical she might do something terrible, injure herself in some way. Skye vividly remembered an incident when they were children: there had been a beautiful doll on the Christmas tree and Jodi had wanted it. When she was told that it was Skye's, a present from her godmother, Jodi had thrown a tantrum, screaming and banging her head against the wall so hard that she had knocked herself silly. But she had got the doll—Aunt Helen had begged it from Skye, promising to buy her another in its place. Another doll had duly arrived, but it had never been the same. Recalling the incident, Skye wondered how Aunt Helen would ever pacify Jodi now—buying a new bridegroom wasn't so easy as buying a doll!

Turning over with a sigh, Skye decided that she should have followed her first instinct and left New York as soon as she could. But Jodi had asked for the portrait, and painting Thane had been too much of a temptation. Skye searched her conscience, trying to decide whether she had let herself be persuaded to do the painting because she had hoped deep down that Thane would want her instead. She hoped not, she hoped she hadn't been so under-hand, but it seemed that when it came to love your mind had little chance of ruling your heart and emotions.

Should she leave now, before it was too late? she wondered. Just make an excuse and go home? Stay away until all this had blown over? It was an easy way out; a coward's way out. Leaving Thane to face everything alone. No, if she loved him, then she must stand by him no matter what.

When the phone rang the next morning, Skye picked up the receiver expecting it to be Thane, but was delighted to hear her mother's voice instead. At first Skye asked a great many eager questions, filled with a sudden wave of nostalgia for her home and family, but her mother's questions weren't so easy to answer, especially the ones about the wedding. She described the bridesmaids' dresses in greater detail than she need have done, then quickly asked about a contract for a calendar she'd been hoping to get. But Anne Holman knew her daughter well and wanted to know what was wrong.

'Well, you mustn't say anything, but I think the wedding is going to be cancelled.'

'Good heavens! Why?'

'Because the bridegroom has changed his mind. He—er—sort of met someone else.'

'I see.' A pause. 'It wasn't you, by any chance?'

'Yes, I'm afraid it was.'

'And are his feelings reciprocated?'

Skye smiled at having what she felt for Thane described so matter-of-factly. 'Yes, they most def-

initely are,' she answered in sudden happy
confidence.

'Oh, dear. Jodi and Helen aren't going to like
that. I take it they don't yet know?'

'No, not yet. At the weekend.'

Her mother asked no more questions and rang
off soon afterwards, but Skye had hardly put the
phone down when it rang again. This time it was
Angie.

'Hi. Have you seen Greenwich Village yet? How
about meeting me there for lunch?'

'Well, I'd love to, but . . .' Skye hesitated.

'Oh, by the way, Thane asked me to give you a
message. He said he'd be along to sit for you tonight as usual.'

'Oh, thanks. And I'd love to meet you for lunch.
Where?'

They arranged a time and place, and at noon
Skye took a cab to Washington Square. They
walked around for a while, Angie pointing out the
old houses that had once belonged to elegant nineteenth-century New Yorkers, then artists and
writers, and were now divided into apartments for
the upwardly mobile. The area had a charm Skye
hadn't found anywhere else in New York, and she
would have been content to wander for much
longer, but Angie's time was limited so they found
a restaurant that specialised in American food with
a touch of the Old South, and ordered chicken pot
pies and delicious home-made bread.

'How's the portrait going?' Angie asked.

'Very well. I might be able to finish it by
tomorrow.'

'And you're pleased with it?'

Skye smiled. 'Yes,' she admitted. 'I'm pleased with it.'

Angie gave her an intent glance and then said casually, 'Thane came home to Maryland last night, after he'd sat for you. He stayed over and brought me into the city this morning.'

'Did he?' Something in Angie's tone made Skye's heart start to beat nervously.

'Uh-huh. And he gave us some pretty shattering news. He said that he was going to break with Jodi and marry you instead.'

'Oh!' Skye blushed scarlet and found it impossible to look at the other girl.

'It was also very welcome news,' Angie added, and grinned at Skye's thunderstruck look. 'My folks wanted me to be sure to tell you that. I guess they fell in love with you, too, when you came down for the weekend.' Leaning forward, Angie said confidentially, 'As a matter of fact, as a family, we weren't very keen on Jodi. My parents never thought she was right for Thane, but...' she shrugged, 'he's a grown man, what can you do?'

'You mean—you mean you don't mind the wedding being called off at this late stage?' Skye said in a daze.

'I told you, they're pleased. And pleased about you. It was pretty obvious at the weekend that Thane was in love with you, you know. He couldn't keep his eyes off you.'

Colour flooded Skye's cheeks again, but she said, 'I'm worried about what's going to happen when Thane tells Jodi at the weekend.'

'I know, especially when you're staying at her parents' apartment. But Mother told me to tell you that you're to come and stay with us. You can come whenever you want. Today, if you like.'

'Oh, Angie, I don't mean I'm worried about me. I'm desperately worried about Jodi. Think what this will do to her.'

The other girl shook her head. 'Quite frankly, I don't think she cares deeply enough about anything to let it spoil her life for very long. Except the wedding itself, of course. She cares about that.'

Skye didn't say anything, but mentally agreed with Angie, realising that it was probably the humiliation of being jilted almost at the church that was going to hurt Jodi the most.

After lunch, when Angie had rushed back to her office, Skye explored on her own for a couple of hours and then went back to the apartment to work. She let herself in and dropped her bag on a chair, then began to walk towards her room when the phone rang. This time it was third time lucky. 'Hi.' Thane's voice sounded warm and near.

'Hello.' Kicking off her shoes, Skye curled up on the settee, holding the receiver close.

'Did you get my message?'

'Yes.'

'And my parents' messages?'

'Yes, those too. They're—they're very kind.'

'They're crazy about you. Told me it's about time I showed some sense.'

'Thane, I haven't said that I . . .'

'I know. So maybe it's about time I taught *you* a little sense,' he said meaningfully.

Skye gave a little gasp, her pulses starting to race. 'That sounds—that sounds...'

Thane laughed. 'Well, c'mon, woman, how does it sound?'

'It sounds wonderful,' she admitted on a sigh. 'But Uncle John?'

'Oh, did I forget to tell you? He tried to call you this afternoon, but you were out, so he left a message with me. He said to tell you he has to entertain a customer tonight and won't be home until very late.'

'Yes, you did forget to tell me that,' Skye said feelingly. 'But, Thane, even so, I don't...' She broke off as there was a ring at the doorbell. 'Oh, there's someone at the door. Hold on.'

Quickly she put down the receiver and ran to the door. 'Who is it?'

'Special delivery, ma'am.'

She went to open the door, but then remembered to look through the spyhole. All she could see was a mass of flowers. Taking off the chain, Skye opened the door, said, 'Would you put them on the table, please?' and turned back to the phone. Then she froze. Catching her breath, she spun round. 'Thane!'

He dropped the personal telephone he'd been using on the table beside the flowers, pushed the door firmly shut and strode towards her. There was no time to protest, no time to say yes. Thane pulled her almost roughly into his arms and bent to kiss her, arching her against him as he took her mouth in a fierce hunger of love and pleading and possession. But, if he had been at all doubtful of how she would react, he was soon reassured. Skye went gladly into his arms, responding to his embrace with all the love and eagerness she'd tried so hard to deny. The room began to sway as she clung to him, each of them muttering frenzied words and endearments against the other's lips, as eager to give as to take.

Thane's mouth left hers as he began to kiss her throat, his lips leaving a searing trail of heat across her skin. 'Oh, Skye, I'm crazy about you. You're beautiful, perfect. Don't fight me any more, my darling. I love you so much, so much.'

Skye leaned back against the strong circle of his arms, her head tilted, moaning softly as his words reached her, the very sound of them a caress. Her breath caught in her throat as he parted the silky material of her blouse and began to kiss the soft, pale skin of the rounded swell of her breasts, and she moved against him, her body on fire. Thane groaned and pulled her close, his hand low on her hips so that she felt the hardness of his body pressing against hers.

'I want you,' he said thickly. 'I want to take your clothes off and look at you. I want to kiss every inch of your body, caress every beautiful part of you. And I want to hold you in my arms all night, every night, for the rest of our lives. I love you, Skye. Please say that you'll marry me, be my wife?'

She smiled and quoted gently. ' "To have and to hold from this day forward." '

'Yes. Oh, yes.' He kissed her again, exploring the softness of her mouth with hungry little kisses that deepened quickly into passion. With a groan,

Thane scooped her up in his arms and carried Skye over to the settee, sat down on it with her across his lap. They kissed then until both of them were trembling and Skye's heart was beating so fast that she could hardly breathe. 'Oh, sweetheart. Sweetheart.' Thane lifted a shaking hand to catch a tear that ran down her cheek. 'What is it? What's the matter?'

Dazedly she shook her head. 'I still can't believe that this is happening. It's like wishing on the moon and having it come true. Oh, Thane, I loved you so, but I never thought that we would be together like this.'

'We'll always be together,' he declared passionately. 'Always. This is for keeps, Skye. I think I knew that from the moment in Nassau when I looked up at the balcony and first saw you. But I couldn't believe it either, at first. Couldn't believe the way I kept thinking about you and wanting to be near you.' His voice sobered suddenly. 'And I couldn't believe that I'd let myself be drawn into making the terrible mistake of getting engaged to Jodi.'

'I feel so guilty about that, about taking you away from her.'

'Don't be. It isn't your fault. It's mine for getting engaged when I wasn't really in love with her.'

'Jodi won't see it like that,' Skye stated in complete certainty. 'She'll blame me.'

'She won't know anything about you. I'll just tell her that I've changed my mind.'

'But is that fair?' Skye ran her fingertip down the cleft in his chin. 'Don't you think she has the right to know?'

'She'll know eventually anyway, but if I just tell her we're through it will give her a chance to get over it before she finds out about you. Don't you think that's better? Kinder?' He ran his lips down her cheek. 'Your skin is so soft. And you smell so sweet. Like a clear new day, like flowers in springtime.'

He kissed the corner of her mouth and she gave a little sighing moan, her lower lip pouting in sensuous arousal. She stirred in his lap and Thane's hold suddenly tightened. He kissed her again, a deep, aching agony of need flaming inside him.

When at last he let her go, Skye's lips felt bruised and there were red marks on her arms where he'd held her. She put her hand against his chest, felt the hammer beat of his heart. 'I want you, Skye,' he muttered against her neck. 'Dear heaven, I've never wanted any woman as I want you.'

Skye smiled and kissed the pulse at his neck, tasted the sweat on his skin. 'I know. I want you, too. But not here. Not in my uncle's home.'

'No.' He looked down at her face, at her soft, pale skin, her mouth parted in unconscious desire, and at the long, dark lashes of her closed eyes. But as he watched her eyes opened and looked intently into his, and he gave a small sigh. 'I guess there are questions you want to ask. Things about me and Jodi that you want to know.'

She shook her head, but sat up straighter as if bracing herself. 'Not unless you want to tell me. I didn't think that the only reason you got engaged to her was because you were on the rebound. There had to be more to it than that.'

'Yeah. Well,' Thane shrugged, 'her attractions are pretty obvious. And she's ornamental. And fun—for a while.'

'You were lovers,' Skye stated. She said it as matter-of-factly as she could, but turned her head away.

'Yes.' Thane lifted her chin so that she had to look at him. 'Do you mind? Does it make any difference?'

'No.' There was a passing moment of regret, and then Skye put it out of her mind forever. 'Did she— were she and Scott lovers, too?'

'Yes.' Thane shrugged. 'Here, if you go with a girl for any length of time, you expect to go to bed together. Isn't it that way in Britain?'

'Yes, I suppose so. If you feel really deeply for someone.' She hesitated, but then answered *his* unspoken question. 'I'm not terribly experienced. You'll have to teach me, I'm afraid.'

'Afraid? Oh, sweetheart, do you think I don't know that? Your innocence shines out of you. It's one of the reasons why I love you so much. And teaching you is going to be the greatest pleasure I've ever known.'

Putting her arms round his neck, Skye smiled into his eyes, her face alight with love. 'I'm kind of looking forward to that myself.' She kissed the cleft in his chin. 'I've been longing to do that.' She bit the lobe of his ear. 'What will you teach me?'

He laughed softly, his hands tightening on her waist. 'You really want to know?'

'Mm.' She kissed him in a sudden surge of desire that took him unawares, but then swung off his lap and got to her feet before he could react.

Her body shaking, she stood with her back to him, but Thane got quickly to his feet and put his hands on her shoulders. 'Skye? Are you OK?'

'Yes.' She turned and let him put his arms around her. 'It all got—got a little too much.' She gave a shaky laugh. 'Maybe you'd better go and sit for me, otherwise this portrait will never get finished.'

He smiled and kissed her nose, his eyes going over her face as if he could never see enough of it. 'OK, if that's what you want.'

It took a while for her to settle to work, but when she did Skye worked well, putting the last touches to his features and his hair. The background could be finished off at any time. After about an hour Skye came to the point when she knew that it was finished, that to add another brushstroke, another highlight, would be over the top. She put down her brush and palette, stood back a little and felt a deep glow of contentment. 'You can come and look now,' she offered.

Thane came to stand beside her, his arm round her waist. Then he looked at the portrait—and caught his breath. It was the best thing she'd ever done, Skye knew that. She had captured all the facets of his character that she loved so much: his determination and thrusting forcefulness, but there was a sense of humour there too, lurking around his mouth. And in his eyes there was anger and

love, both, but whereas anger had been the pre-
dominant feature, now, after tonight, it was love.

Slowly Thane let out his breath in a low whistle
of admiration. 'Skye, you're wasting your talent
on the work you're doing. You should be painting
pictures like this. It's—it's just great,' he said
unsteadily.

'No. It's because it was painted with love. And
fear. And hope.' Her voice grew a little sad. 'I
wonder what will happen to it now. When you tell
Jodi, she might not want it. If there's to be no
wedding . . .'

'Maybe we'll be able to keep it,' Thane finished
for her. 'I hope we can. I think it tells us both so
much. If you'd let me see it before, I'm sure I would
have known how you felt about me.'

'But you did, surely?' Skye said, turning to put
her arms loosely round his neck, her slim hips
touching his.

'I was pretty sure you liked me, but more than
that I wasn't really certain. You seemed to be getting
on OK with Scott—and you seemed to deliberately
avoid me those last couple of weekends in Nassau.'

'I tried—but it wasn't easy,' she confessed.

'No, it wasn't easy. I tried, too. But those
weekends made me realise how much I cared about
you. I missed talking to you, being near you. I realised that I was in love with you. And it made me
feel like a boy again—a timid sixteen-year-old who
was in love for the very first time. I felt vulnerable
and afraid. Yes, afraid,' he insisted when Skye
raised her eyebrows in disbelief. 'Afraid that you
didn't care for me. That there might be some man

back in England that you were in love with. I can't remember the last time I felt so unsure of myself, so afraid that you'd turn round and tell me to go to hell.'

'Oh, Thane!' Skye held him tighter and glanced at the portrait. 'If Jodi hadn't asked me to do this picture, we might not have seen each other again until the wedding. I was all set to leave New York a couple of weeks ago. I just—just had to get away. I couldn't bear to see you and Jodi together any longer.'

'You were going to take off? Where?'

'Anywhere.' She gave a shaky laugh. 'Not that it would really have helped much; I'd still have pictured you in my mind.'

'But that's all behind us now. We found each other and that's all that matters. Everything's going to be fine from now on.' Lifting his hand, he stroked her cheek tenderly, then bent to kiss her— a long kiss of gladness and gratitude.

When he at length raised his head, Skye stood with her eyes closed for a moment, as if reluctant to return to reality, but then she opened them and suddenly gave a great shiver and clung to him. 'Hold me close. Please hold me close.' And when he put his arms round her she looked up at him with wide, scared eyes. 'Oh, Thane, I love you so much. So very much. It makes me afraid.'

'Afraid? Why?'

'We ought not to feel so happy. Not when Jodi is going to be hurt so badly. I can't help feeling that something terrible will happen. That this is all too wonderful to be true. I felt so cold suddenly, as if someone had walked over my grave.'

'Hey, now, that's crazy. Haven't I said that everything's going to be fine? Trust me. OK? The only terrible thing that's going to happen to you is that you're going to have to marry me—and soon. I want to go to bed with you and wake up with you beside me for the rest of my life.'

Skye smiled, immediately reassured. 'You'll have to come to England and meet my family first,' she warned.

'Will you put in a good word for me?'

She gave him a provocative look. 'I might—if suitably persuaded.'

Thane grinned and tightened his grip on her waist. 'Oh, yeah? Well, in that case, how's this for starters?'

He drew her against him, the laughter in his eyes fading as they darkened with desire. He lowered his head to kiss her, but their lips had hardly touched when there was the sound of a key being turned in the lock, and they quickly drew apart as Uncle John came in.

'Hi. How did the meeting go?'

Thane stepped in front of Skye, placing himself between her and John Benton to give her a chance to hide the rush of colour that flooded her cheeks. Reaching up, she drew the cloth that she'd used over the portrait, not wanting anyone else to see it yet. Somehow she managed to greet Uncle John, but Thane helped by drawing him into conversation for the ten minutes or so before he left, and then she made the excuse that she wanted to wash her hair and went to her room.

That night she lay in bed, wanting to relive every second of the evening with Thane, but instead fell almost instantly asleep and didn't wake until after Uncle John had left. Thane rang at ten and they arranged to meet for lunch, but both found that they were only hungry for each other's company, and so they spent the time strolling hand in hand through Central Park, past the zoo and along the lake.

'I always thought that this place was dangerous,' Skye remarked as they paused in the shade of a tree. 'But it's full of people and everything is so peaceful.'

'It's safe enough at this southern end below the Metropolitan Museum during the day, but at night it's dangerous. All the winos and drug addicts come here then.'

They walked on for a while in the sun, but then Thane said abruptly, 'Jodi called me last night. She wanted to know why I haven't been in touch.'

Skye came to a stop and turned to look at him with troubled eyes. 'What did you say?'

'I made an excuse, said I'd been loaded down with work. Or at least I started to. Then I knew that I couldn't go on like this any longer. I had to tell her the truth.'

'You told her over the phone?' she asked in a shocked voice.

He gave a sharp negative shake of his head. 'No. But I told her that I had to see her. I'm flying down to Nassau this afternoon, and I've asked Jodi to meet me at the airport.'

'Oh, Thane!'

There was fear in her voice, but he knew that it wasn't for herself. 'Don't worry. She'll be fine. After I've told her, I'll call her mother and explain, then put Jodi in a cab. It has to be done, Skye,' he added roughly.

'Yes, I know. When—when will you be back?'

'Tonight. I'm going to catch the same plane back to New York. It's better that way. There's no sense in hanging it out.'

'No, I suppose not.

They came to the Fifth Avenue entrance, and Thane stopped and took her hands. 'The next time I see you I'll be free.'

For a moment Skye was too choked to speak, could only clasp his hands tightly, but then she said, 'I can't stay at the apartment, not after you tell Jodi: she might come there, might even want to talk to me about it. Perhaps she'll even ask me if I know why!'

'I know, I've thought of that. I want you out of it, too. But it will be better if you don't come to my place yet, so I've arranged for you to stay at a friend's apartment. He's on holiday on the coast with his wife and kids for the summer. I rang him today and he's going to call the janitor of his building and tell him to let you have a key. You can move in tonight. Here's the address.' He smiled and bent to kiss her nose. 'And I'll be round to-morrow evening.'

There was a warmth of promise in his voice that brought a flush to Skye's cheeks, but she said anxiously, 'And you'll call me and let me know how things went with Jodi?'

'Sure. But it'll be OK. You'll see. Now I have to go, sweetheart, if I'm going to catch that plane. I have to call at my apartment first to pick up my passport.' Putting his hand on her neck, he kissed her with fierce longing, then turned abruptly and stepped to the kerb to hail a cab. One pulled up almost immediately, and Skye stood and watched it drive away, lifting her hand to return his wave from the rear window.

With nothing to do but worry for the rest of the day, Skye went to the Museum of Modern Art and tried to lose herself in the paintings, but was too anxious to concentrate. She kept looking at her watch, trying to work out what time Thane would arrive in Nassau, how long he would spend with Jodi, and what time he would get back. She walked round galleries and museums until her feet gave out, then took a cab back to the apartment and began to pack her cases. That done, she took notice of the noises in her stomach and thought she'd better go and eat. Skye stretched out the meal for as long as she could, sitting at a booth in a cafeteria and not taking much notice of what she ate. At eight she decided that it must be all over by now, and Thane possibly on his way home.

She paid her bill and took the address Thane had given her from her purse. Perhaps it would be better if she went there first and got the key. The apartment turned out to be near Greenwich Village, and was modern but pleasantly cluttered with left-behind toys and books. There was also a very big bed in the master bedroom. The janitor turned on the air-conditioning for her and warned that the ice-box was empty. So Skye went to a nearby store, amazed that it was still open so late, and bought a bag of groceries which she took back to the new apartment, which already began to feel agreeably cool.

It was almost ten by the time that was done, and there was nothing left but to go back to her uncle's place and collect her things. And also tell him that she was moving out. He would, of course, want an explanation and she would have to lie, to think up an excuse to satisfy him. But if Jodi or Aunt Helen had telephoned him from Nassau, then maybe he would have gone down there and she could just leave a note.

But as soon as Skye opened the door of the apartment she knew he was there because the lights were on. She braced herself to meet him and stepped into the room, closing the door behind her. 'Uncle John? I . . .' But then she became very still. There was only one person in the room, and it wasn't her uncle. Jodi stood at the far end of the room, in front of the easel. She had thrown the cover off and was gazing at Thane's portrait. 'Jodi! But I thought you were in Nassau. I . . .' Skye stopped in confusion.

'Yes, I was,' Jodi agreed in a remote kind of voice. 'But Mummy and I chartered a plane and flew up here.' She was still looking at the portrait, gazing at it as if hypnotised.

'Is—is Aunt Helen here?'

'No, she and Daddy have gone to Thane's place to talk to him. To ask him why he has jilted me,' she said in sudden harsh, grating bitterness. Then she turned to look at Skye. 'But they needn't have bothered, need they? It's all here in this picture. It's because of you. You've seduced him.' Her voice rose hysterically until she was suddenly screaming. 'You rotten bitch! You took advantage of me not being here, and you seduced my fiancé behind my back!'

CHAPTER EIGHT

FOR a long moment the two girls just stared at each other, the silence as shattering as the screamed accusation. Then Skye said wretchedly, 'Oh, Jodi, I'm sorry. I'm so terribly sorry.'

'Sorry?' The other girl spat the word back at her. 'You liar. You planned this. You probably planned it all along.'

'No, that isn't true. We tried to fight it. We didn't want to hurt you. Please, Jodi, you've got to believe . . .'

'Shut up! I don't want to hear your lies. You're not having him, do you hear me? Thane is *mine*. And we're going to be married in Nassau, just as we planned. I'm *not* going to let a stupid, insipid tart like you make a laughing-stock of me. So you can just clear out of here and go back to England. *Now*.'

Skye, her face full of concern, went up to Jodi and tried to put a hand on her arm, but her cousin shook it off violently. 'Jodi, please try to understand. Nobody planned this. It just happened. Surely Thane told you that?'

'Oh, he told me lots of things, back there in that squalid little cafeteria in Nassau airport,' Jodi answered viciously. 'He said it was better to break now rather than after we were married. But he didn't tell me about *you*, you bitch! But then I'm sure you instructed him not to. You wanted to keep out of it, didn't you? After all, you have been living in my parents' houses, taking their hospitality, while all the time you've been seducing their future son-in-law,' Jodi added in sneering bitterness.

Skye winced, but said steadily, 'I was going to leave; I just came back to collect my things.'

'To move in with Thane, I suppose. Good Lord, I don't know what the hell he sees in you. I bet you're hopeless in bed.' She turned suddenly, strode over to the bar and helped herself from an already open bottle of brandy. The drink seemed to steady her a little because she seemed more purposeful, but just as bitter as she snarled out, 'I suppose you think you're in love with him. Well, let me tell you, if Thane marries you it will be the biggest mistake in his life. He has a brilliant future ahead of him, could even make it into politics. And he needs the kind of wife who's going to help him and encourage him. Not some dewy-eyed little doormat who only wants to stay home and have kids. Do you understand what I'm saying? If you marry him, he's finished careerwise. And he'll grow to hate you for it. OK, maybe he fancies you now, but he sure won't in ten years' time when he sees everyone else getting ahead but he's saddled with a drag like you!'

Her voice slurred over several words in her angry tirade, and Skye realised that the medicinal brandy hadn't been the first one Jodi had had. Slowly, trying to keep things calm, Skye said, 'Tell me, Jodi, why were you going to marry Thane? Because you loved him—or because he had all the prospects of a future in politics? Did you see yourself as the wife of a governor? Or perhaps even higher than that, in Washington itself? Were you marrying him to further his ambition—or was it your own? What about now? Don't you love him for what he is now? Suppose something happened to him a month after you were married and he couldn't work any more. What would you do then? Divorce him? Leave him?' Anger came, momentarily replacing pity. 'Well, I love him for himself, Jodi, not for what he might be in twenty years' time. And I'm sorry, but I'm not going to give him up.'

'And his career—what about that? He'll never get anywhere with you. He...'

'Whatever he wants to do is fine by me,' Skye broke in. 'I'll help him in any way I can. He will always come before my own work. But I'm not going to tell him how to live his life, and I'm not going to live *through* him.'

Her firmness seemed to get through to Jodi at last. She stared at Skye, her usually immaculate hair uncombed, her make-up smudged and her eyes red from crying. As she realised the inevitable, she seemed to shrivel and look haggard. Immediately Skye's soft heart was filled with pity and she again went up to her. 'Jodi, come and sit down. Let me make you a coffee. I...'

'No!' Jodi's eyes suddenly dilated with anger and she hit out at Skye, striking her across the face.

Skye staggered back dizzily, but then gave a cry as Jodi grabbed the painting from the easel. 'No! Don't.'

She made a grab for the picture, but Jodi swung it out of the way and smashed it against the wall. 'You're not going to have him,' she screamed. 'He's going to marry me! Me! Me!'

As she screamed she brought the picture crashing down on the table, the television set, a chair, trying to destroy it. The telephone began to ring, but stopped almost immediately as the picture caught it and the receiver went flying off the hook.

'Jodi, don't, please.'

But Jodi gave a cry of triumph as the canvas finally split and she was able to get hold of the frayed edges and tear it to shreds. Then she turned on Skye, laughing hysterically. 'And now I'm going to deal with you.'

Skye braced herself to fend her off, but Jodi ran to her father's desk and pulled out the bottom drawer so violently that all the contents fell on the floor. She scrabbled among them—and came up holding a gun.

Again a silence of tension filled the room. Skye stared at the gun incredulously, unable to believe that Jodi would go that far. She was standing near the fallen telephone receiver and could hear noises coming from it. So maybe they could hear her. 'Is—is that a real gun?' she demanded, trying to speak loudly and clearly, but not succeeding very well.

'Of course it's real. My father keeps it to protect us from burglars. And now you're going to do what I want.'

'What—what do you mean?' The noises coming from the telephone had stopped, and Skye could only pray that someone had heard and was on their way to help. She must play for time, keep Jodi talking as much as she could.

But Jodi only said shortly, 'You'll find out. Now get going,' and she gestured towards the door.

'Jodi, this isn't going to help.'

She tried to persuade Jodi to put the gun down, cajoling, pleading, but the other girl only laughed, then got angry again. 'Go on, do as you're told,' she threatened.

Slowly Skye went to the door. There was no one in the corridor outside. Jodi made her press the button for the elevator and, when they got in, press it again to go down to the basement where the cars were garaged. Jodi unlocked her father's car and said, 'OK, get in. And don't try anything.'

Skye obeyed in a kind of daze. It's like a film, she thought. Or a dream. Maybe I'll wake up in a minute and none of this will have happened.

Jodi put the keys in the ignition and started the car, but realised she couldn't drive with the gun in her hand. A look of uncertainty came into her eyes, and Skye tried to persuade her to go back to the apartment, but any persuasion seemed only to make Jodi angrier. 'Shut up.' She bit her lip in indecision, and Skye was sure she had no idea what to do, but she suddenly made up her mind and swung the car out of the underground garage and up to the street. She pulled out immediately after a car that shot past towards the front of the building but then came to a halt suddenly, its tyres screaming. Jodi turned in the other direction, fast but erratically, as she tried to cope with the gun and the steering-wheel.

It was dark now, or as dark as it would ever be in such a brilliantly lit city as New York. There was a lot of other traffic on the streets, people going home from theatres and restaurants, and there were police cars too. Skye saw one, and for a moment contemplated grabbing the wheel to swerve the car and attract their attention. But that would be no good, it would only make things even worse for Jodi than they were already. Skye didn't feel so guilty about Thane now, but there was no way she was going to get her cousin into trouble with the police. She peered out of the window, trying to see where they were, and recognised some of the stores in Fifth Avenue. Then Jodi took a right and turned into Central Park.

The road was well-lit, and Skye thought they were going to go across the park and out the other side, but Jodi turned into one of the smaller roads that honeycombed the park, and then on to another, until they were in a dark area with hardly any lights. 'Now get out,' Jodi yelled. 'Go on, get out.'

Skye stared at her in horror. 'You can't mean it.'

'Yes, I do. I'll teach you to steal my fiancé! To ruin my wedding!'

'Jodi, please.' Desperately now, Skye tried to argue, but the other girl waved the gun in her face, and she realised that Jodi was just unhinged enough by shock and anger to use it. Slowly, reluctantly, Skye got out of the car. Jodi instantly drove away, heading fast towards the lighted road.

The night was very warm, but Skye felt cold with terror as she stood alone in the darkness, desperately trying to probe the shadows. She didn't know where the nearest gate was, which way to go to people and light and safety. A sound came from her left and made her mind up for her. Skye turned and bolted to the right, relying on her youth and fitness to outrun the pounding steps that came after her. Her own heart was beating so loudly that she couldn't hear if she was still being chased, but then she ran into a tree and went sprawling on the ground. She lay there, dazed, wondering desperately if she would ever get out of this place. Then she heard it—in the dim distance someone was calling her name. At first she was convinced that it was only in her head, but then it came again and she recognised Thane's voice. Getting to her feet, Skye began to run towards the sound, trying to keep in the shadows, to go from one tree to the next.

Twice she went in the wrong direction and the sound faded, so that Skye had to turn and try again. He must be in his car, perhaps cruising slowly along, she realised. Once she opened her mouth to call him, but shut it with a snap when she saw a group of men sitting and lying beside a bench, passing bottles between them. She had to circle round them carefully, and by then she couldn't hear Thane's voice at all. She came to a building, a closed-up hamburger stall from the smell that still hung about it, and paused to still the panic-beating of her heart. Desperately she listened for Thane's call, but there was only the distant sound of the great city, and nearer voices raised in anger, swearing and cursing, and the low moaning of a man whimpering in his sleep.

About fifty yards ahead she could see the tarmac gleam of a road, unlit because the lamps had all been smashed. If she followed the road it must lead eventually to the more brightly lit areas and she could stop a car, ask for a lift. But that might be dangerous, too. Her straining ears caught stealthy sounds moving towards her, coming not from one direction but at least three different points. The hairs on the back of her neck pricked in fear as

Skye gave a sob of terror. Looking over her shoulder, she saw the white blobs of faces as they suddenly began to rush towards her. At the same time the headlights of a car came into view along the unlit road. Choosing the lesser of two evils, Skye sprang forward and began to run. A hand caught her sleeve and she cried out but plunged on, the thin material tearing easily. She ran then as she had never run before, leaping on to the road and running towards the car, her arms held wide to make it stop.

It screeched to a halt only a couple of feet in front of her, the back of the car rising and bucking as the brakes were slammed on. Skye ran to the passenger door and wrenched it open. 'Oh, please. Please will you . . .' And then she gave a great gasp of joy. 'Thane!'

'Get in, quick.'

His yell galvanised her. Skye fell in the car and Thane gunned the engine, just as several men began to crowd round and try to hem it in. He had to reverse, the engine screaming, until he was far enough away to turn and head back to the main road.

'Skye, are you OK? Oh, hell, Skye.' As soon as they were in a safe enough place, Thane stopped the car and reached for her, gathering her trembling body into his arms.

She clung to him, tears of relief wetting her cheeks. 'I thought you'd gone. I heard you, but I couldn't get to you in time. And then those men came.'

'Did they touch you? Did they hurt you?'

'No. No, but I was so scared.'

Thane held her, kissed her, comforted her, letting her feel the safety and strength of his closeness, murmuring words of reassurance until he was seized with a sudden burst of anger. 'I'm going to kill Jodi for this! Anything could have happened to you out there.'

Her trembling had largely stopped now, and Skye lifted a hand to touch his face. 'How did you know I was there?'

'Jodi's father called her from my apartment to make sure she was OK and we heard what was going on, so I got over there as fast as I could and just saw you and Jodi driving away. I had to turn to follow you, and I lost you until I realised she'd turned into the park. Then I passed her leaving that northern area alone, and I knew you were in there somewhere.'

'Oh, Thane, if you hadn't come——'

'It's OK. Everything's going to be fine.' He kissed her again, brushing her hair gently back from her face, his anger increasing at the remembered terror in her eyes. 'C'mon. I'm going to take you back to my place so you can have a hot bath and sleep this off.'

'Yes, but can we go back to Uncle John's apartment first? I have to know what's happened to Jodi.'

'After all she's done to you? Why, she . . .'

'After all *we've* done to her,' Skye pointed out gently. 'Please, Thane, I have to know.'

He looked at her for a moment, then nodded. 'Yes, I guess you're right.'

Skye hadn't known what she would have to face when they reached the apartment, but she certainly hadn't expected to find any policemen there. But there were two, with one of the building's security men, talking to her aunt and uncle, who were both obviously upset. When Aunt Helen saw Skye hesitating in the open doorway, she ran forward with a cry and grabbed Skye's arm. 'Where's Jodi? What have you done with her?'

'You mean, what has Jodi done?' Thane burst out angrily, but then stopped, realising that the policemen were listening. 'Why are they here?'

'A neighbour saw our door open and thought we'd been burgled. She told the security man, who called the police.'

'I'm afraid that was my fault,' Skye said clearly. 'I went out in a hurry and forgot to close the door.'

'What about this?' a policeman asked, gesturing to the remains of Thane's portrait, and all the things Jodi had knocked down or broken in her efforts to destroy it.

'Oh—er—I'm afraid that was just a fit of temper, nothing more.'

'You British?' the policeman asked, coming over to her. Skye admitted that she was, and he gave her a short but pointed lecture on security, and then the three men all left amid profuse apologies and thanks from Uncle John.

As soon as they'd gone, John Benton demanded to know what had happened, and went grey when Skye told him. 'She left you in the park?'

'Yes. But—but I'm afraid she still has your gun,' Skye added wretchedly.

But to her surprise he said, 'It's only loaded with blanks. I just kept it to scare anyone who might break in.'

'I wish I'd known that,' Skye said feelingly.

Her aunt turned on her in sudden fury. 'If you hadn't come here, none of this would have happened.' She went to go on, but just then the phone rang and she ran to answer it, her face clearing like magic as she listened. 'It's all right. It's Scott. Jodi went to him and he's bringing her back here. He's phoning from his car and is on his way now.'

'Do you want to leave now?' Thane asked Skye.

She shook her head. 'I must be sure she's all right first.'

'OK.' Thane's mouth twisted derisively. 'I told you she'd go to Scott—straight to the next available man.'

'How dare you speak about my daughter like that?' Aunt Helen shouted angrily. 'It's all because of you that...'

But Uncle John caught her arm and said tartly, 'For heaven's sake, Helen! We both know he's right. Jodi's been spoilt, that's the trouble. Don't you realise what she's done by abandoning Skye in the park? If Skye had been raped or murdered, Jodi would have gone to prison. Prison, do you understand?'

'She wasn't herself,' Aunt Helen protested loyally. 'Any girl would be unhinged for a while after the shock of being jilted.' And she shot a venomous look at Thane.

'You should be grateful that Skye didn't tell the police,' Uncle John said, so sharply that his wife gave him a rather stunned look. Taking her arm, he led her into the far corner of the room and began to remonstrate with her so strongly that she was soon silenced.

Thane glanced at them, and then stooped down to pick up what was left of the portrait. 'I suppose by destroying this, Jodi felt that she was destroying me,' he said shortly. 'I'm sorry, sweetheart. It was a brilliant painting.'

'It doesn't matter. I . . .'

But before Skye could go on there was a ring at the doorbell, and they all turned as Uncle John went to open it, expecting to see Jodi and Scott. But the caller was a man by himself, a tall, good-looking man of about thirty with thick, dark hair that fell forward on to his forehead. To Thane he was a complete stranger, but Skye gave a gasp, her face lightening, and pulled her hand from Thane's to run forward and throw herself into the stranger's arms.

'James! Oh, James, I'm so glad you're here.'

'Mother phoned to say she thought you were in trouble.' James Holman looked round at the disordered room. 'It seems she was right.' He greeted the Bentons and then turned to Thane, his eyes assessing him. 'You must be Thane Tyson. I'm Skye's brother.'

Thane grinned. 'Well, that's a relief. I was beginning to get a bit worried there.'

'What's been happening here?'

Thane had just finished explaining when Scott and Jodi arrived. Jodi had obviously been crying again, and there was a frightened look in her eyes that gave way to relief as soon as she saw Skye. 'I told you she'd be all right. I . . .' She broke off suddenly as she saw James. 'James? But how did you . . .?' She turned away, her face very white.

'Darling, are you all right?' Her mother rushed to put her arms round her.

'Yes. Yes, I'm OK.' Jodi looked over her shoulder at James, an unhappy, almost tentative expression on her face, but then she saw Thane and her features hardened. Striding over to where they were standing, she pulled off her engagement ring and threw it at Thane's feet. 'Here, take your two-bit ring. As far as I'm concerned, she's welcome to you. I don't know why I bothered with you in the first place. I always did prefer Scott. He has far more drive than you'll ever have.' And she went to link her arms possessively in Scott's.

But he gave a rueful sort of sigh and gently disengaged his arm. 'Sorry, Jodi, but Angie and I are—well, serious about each other. We really feel we have something going for us this time.'

Jodi flinched, her face whiter than ever. She seemed so intensely alone that Skye's heart was filled with compassion and she went to go to her, but James put his hand on her arm to stop her. 'Better let me handle it,' he said, and walked over to Jodi. 'Hello, coz. I'm thirsty—how about making a weary traveller a cup of coffee?' He put a casual hand on Jodi's shoulder as he spoke, and she trembled, so violently that they could all see it. She gave him a swift, uncertain glance and then nodded and led the way to the kitchen.

There was a momentary silence when they'd gone, until Scott crossed to Uncle John and held out the gun. 'I believe this is yours, sir. As a lawyer, I'd advise you to either get rid of it or keep it locked away. Goodnight.' He nodded to Aunt Helen, then came over to Skye and Thane. 'Glad you're OK,' he said to Skye, and kissed her on the cheek. 'And as for you, buddy...' He punched Thane's arm. 'Congratulations.'

'And to you,' Thane grinned.

They shook hands, and as soon as Scott had left Thane turned to Skye. She nodded at the question in his raised eyebrows. 'I'll get my things, I'm all packed.'

She went into the bedroom and came out with her case and a large square parcel which Thane took from her. 'I'll just leave a note for James, let him know where I'll be.' She wrote down the address and telephone number of the apartment near Greenwich Village and took it into the kitchen. They were sitting drinking coffee, and the lost look was fading from Jodi's eyes as she listened to James's story of some of the places he'd been to during his job as a reporter. Jodi looked away when Skye came in, but James gave her an encouraging wink and a thumbs-up sign as she gave him the address.

Then came the hard part, having to say goodbye to her aunt and uncle. She started to say, 'I'm so sorry. We really didn't want to...' when Thane interrupted.

'You don't have to apologise, Skye. I've already said everything that has to be said. Goodnight, sir. Ma'am.' And Skye only had time to grab her bag before he was ushering her out to the car.

'Wow! I'm glad that's over. Somehow I don't think my aunt and uncle will ever want to see me again.'

'Yeah, it's been a heck of a day.' Skye leaned against his shoulder as he began to drive. 'My place?'

She shook her head. 'No, your friend's place.'

'Good. It's nearer.'

It was so late by now that there was very little traffic on the road, and they reached the apartment in just a few minutes. Skye switched on a lamp and turned to Thane, feeling suddenly shy. 'It's—it's a very nice flat. Are you sure your friends won't mind us using it?'

'Quite sure. Skye.' He held out his hands and she ran to him.

'Oh, Thane. I love you so much.'

He kissed her wildly, almost desperately. 'I thought I'd lost you. I never want to go through such hell again.' Putting his hands on either side of her face, he rained kisses down on her mouth, her eyes, her cheeks. 'You scared the hell out of me. When I was driving round the park looking for you, the most terrible pictures were going through my mind.'

They kissed fervently, each seeking and giving reassurance until Thane held her close against his hardening body, his kisses deepening into passion and awareness. 'I ought to go away and let you get some sleep,' he said thickly. 'You must be exhausted.'

'Mm. Maybe it would be better if you left.'

Thane straightened up, trying to hide his disappointment. 'OK. I'll call you tomorrow.' He kissed her again and went reluctantly to the door, but turned as she said his name.

Skye stood there laughing at him. 'You idiot. Of course I'm not tired. I've never been more awake in my life. And if you leave me now I'll never speak to you again.' Her voice grew husky. 'Because I want all those things you said, too. I want you to undress me and take me to bed and make love to me and...oh!'

She gave an exclamation of surprise as Thane suddenly strode over to her, scooped her up in his arms and carried her into the bedroom. He kissed her fiercely, his hands going to the buttons of her dress. 'You minx. Is this what you want? And this?' Her dress fell to the floor, followed by the wispy lace of her bra.

Skye cried out, her hands digging into his shoulders as his lips touched her skin, setting her body on fire, her nerve-ends flaming into awareness. His panting, ragged breath was a fire in itself, making her gasp and writhe as the deep ache of desire uncurled through her body. She cried out his name as Thane kissed her breasts and pulled at his clothes, wanting to be closer still. A great shudder ran through her as he held her against his bare chest, his skin damp with the heat of anticipation and longing. He kissed her neck, her throat, his hands caressing her avidly.

'You're so lovely. So beautiful. Dear heaven, Skye, I want you so badly.'

Lifting her hands, she stroked them across his chest, felt the hammering of his heart. 'And I you, my love.' She kissed him tenderly, yieldingly, in a kiss that was deeper than passion.

Afterwards he groaned, his mouth against her throat, and carried her to the big bed. He took off the rest of her clothes and then the rest of his own, and stood looking down at her for a long moment, trying to hold this instant of time in his memory forever. But then Skye held out her arms and he came down beside her, loving her, caressing her, lifting her to the dizzy heights of excitement as he finally made love in a need so desperate that he lost control and took her in a blaze of wild, abandoned passion.

Gentleness came later, much later, when their eager craving had been satisfied more than once and there was time to whisper words of tenderness, to touch and explore, to marvel and caress, to make love slowly, tenderly, revelling in the joy and pleasure they gave each other.

When they finally fell asleep, close in each other's arms, it was already daylight and the city was coming to life, the skyscrapers casting long shadows over the streets and now innocent-looking park as the sun rose in the sky, promising another hot and glorious day. They slept on until the insistent note of the telephone woke them and Thane sat up, his face breaking into a smile of happy awareness as he saw where he was and that Skye was beside him. He kissed her soft, love-sated lips and picked up the phone. 'Hello?' His eyebrows rose and he held out the receiver. 'It's for you. Your brother.'

Skye sat up, pulling the sheet over her chest. Thane immediately pulled it down again and she gave him an indignant look. 'Hello, James. No, of course you didn't wake us—me. Where are you?' She listened, and then caught her breath as Thane's hand began to caress her, his skilful fingers bringing her body wide awake. 'No, it's nothing. Go on.' She caught Thane's hand, her eyes widening. 'She's what? James are you sure you know what you're doing? Why, yes, I know, but...' She listened some more, then said, 'Well, if you're sure...I wish you

luck. Be sure and let me know how you get on.'
Her cheeks suddenly filled with fiery colour and
she glanced at Thane. 'Yes, he did, as a matter of
fact. More so. Goodbye.'

'What was that all about?' Thane demanded.

'Wow!' Skye leaned back against the pillows.
'James has persuaded Jodi to go to Africa with him
while he covers the famine there. He said it will do
her good to rough it in a tent and see how the Third
World people live.'

'Jodi in a tent? She'll be back in Nassau within
a week.'

'I don't know. James can be very forceful when
he wants to be. If Jodi isn't completely spoilt, then
I think he's the man to bring out the better side of
her character. And they always did like each other
before Uncle John got rich and they went to live
in Nassau.'

'It's going to be a tough lesson.'

'Mm. But she might even enjoy it—with James.'

Thane grinned. 'Talking about lessons, there's
something else I wanted to teach you.'

Skye laughed and kissed him, but pushed him
firmly away. 'Later. Now I'm going to have a
shower and a huge breakfast, which *you* are going
to help make.'

'Tyrant,' Thane complained in complete contentment, and watched her admiringly as she walked
across to the bathroom.

The sun shone through a high, arched window
on to the table where they sat to eat their belated
breakfast, both wrapped in borrowed bathrobes.
They sat close, their eyes full of happiness and love
as they looked often at each other. But when they'd

finished their coffee Thane said regretfully, 'You know, there's only one thing that stops our happiness from being complete.'

'What's that?'

'That Jodi destroyed that portrait. Even if you painted another, it would never be the same, never as good. That picture had all the emotion in it that we were feeling then: unspoken love, desire.'

Skye laughed. 'In that case, you can be perfectly happy, because...' She went to where Thane had put her things the night before, and picked up the parcel, eagerly pulling off the wrapper. 'Here it is. Your portrait. And finished.' And she held up the painting with Thane now against a background of a flame tree as she'd seen him in Nassau.

Thane stared and got to his feet. 'But Jodi destroyed it!'

'No.' She shook her head. 'Jodi destroyed the copy that I'd been working on that morning. I'm afraid I was going to give that one to her and keep the original for myself. I started it before we—well, realised we were in love. I wanted it because I thought you were going to marry Jodi and I might never see you again!'

'Idiot.' Thane kissed her on the nose and took the picture from her to stand it on a table against the wall. 'You must paint a self-portrait to go with it. Was the copy very similar?'

'Enough for Jodi to recognise that we were in love.'

'Ah, I wondered how she knew. I didn't tell either her or her parents.'

'I'm glad she saw. I was finding it very difficult to hide how I felt about you.'

'And I you.' Thane kissed her with growing passion, then picked her up in his arms.

Skye's eyes widened. 'Again?'

'Well, you did say later,' he pointed out. 'And I take it that you're a woman who keeps her promises.'

'Always,' Skye breathed, and smiled mistily up at him. 'To you, always and always and always.'

Harlequin Presents®

Coming Next Month

#1279 FLAWLESS Sara Craven
As a gawky, plain teenager, Carly had suffered bitter disillusion at the hands of Saul Kingsland. And she had vowed to get her revenge. Now, as an acknowledged beauty and successful model, she was finally ready to destroy him.

#1280 GOODBYE FOREVER Sandra Field
Roslin was trying to escape from a life that had suddenly turned sour. Tyson had a past that made him scared to trust the future. A chance meeting brought them together, and their paths seemed fated to cross. They both deserved a little happiness. Could they find it together?

#1281 A HEART AS BIG AS TEXAS Emma Goldrick
Stedman Colson behaved like a perfect neighbor when he moved in next door to Alison Springer. Too perfect perhaps. The local sheriff was very interested in her activities—and Stedman was, after all, a lawyer. But whose side was he on?

#1282 BEYOND COMPARE Penny Jordan
Holly was determined to make Howard Neston appreciate what he lost in jilting her for Rosamund, and Drew Hammond was the ideal man to help her—after all, Rosamund had jilted _him_ for Howard. It was logical for Holly and Drew to pretend to be lovers to make the other couple jealous.

#1283 ISLAND TURMOIL Annabel Murray
Chryssanti's puppy love for her cousin Christos was part of the past. But recently married Christos didn't believe it—and neither did his brother Dimitri. And Chrys was beginning to find that Dimitri's distrust hurt her far more than she'd ever dreamed.

#1284 A BEWITCHING COMPULSION Susan Napier
Clare had enough trouble preventing her mother-in-law from exploiting her son Tim's talent as a violin prodigy. But to be under attack from maestro David Deverenko was too much—especially when he turned his interest to Clare herself.

#1285 THE SEAL WIFE Eleanor Rees
Cathy's domestic services agency had met its first failure in the obnoxious Adam Dale, but she was resigned to it. That was, until the famous author Nick Ballantyn persuaded her that his friend Adam and his teenage daughter really did need her at their remote Yorkshire farmhouse.

#1286 DANGEROUS OBSESSION Patricia Wilson
Since her foster brother Dan had so cruelly dashed her hopes of winning his love, Anna had done her best to eliminate her obsession with him. She had nearly succeeded—until he suddenly returned from the Bahamas and crashed back into the forefront of her life.

Available in June wherever paperback books are sold, or through Harlequin Reader Service:

In the U.S.
901 Fuhrmann Blvd.
P.O. Box 1397
Buffalo, N.Y. 14240-1397

In Canada
P.O. Box 603
Fort Erie, Ontario
L2A 5X3

Take 4 bestselling love stories FREE

Plus get a FREE surprise gift!

Harlequin Superromance

A June title
not to be missed....

Superromance author Judith Duncan has created her
most powerfully emotional novel yet, a book about
love too strong to forget and hate too painful to
remember....

Risen from the ashes of her past like a phoenix,
Sydney Foster knew too well the price of wisdom,
especially that gained in the underbelly of the city.
She'd sworn she'd never go back, but in order to
embrace a future with the man she loved, she had to
return to the streets...and settle an old score.

Once in a long while, you read a book that affects you
so strongly, you're never the same again. Harlequin is
proud to present such a book, STREETS OF FIRE by
Judith Duncan (Superromance #407). Her book merits
Harlequin's AWARD OF EXCELLENCE for June 1990,
conferred each month to one specially selected title.

S407-1